Memory in Lockdown:
Creative Nonfiction

Edited by Sandra Joy and Alexandra Lewis

First published in 2021 by Hunter Writers Centre, Newcastle, Australia

Co-edited by Sandra Joy and Alexandra Lewis
Cover illustration by Hannah McGregor

First Printed in Australia by Lightning Source

National Library of Australian Cataloguing-in-Publication entry:

A catalogue record for this
work is available from the
National Library of Australia

Title: Memory in Lockdown: Creative Nonfiction
Audience: Young Adult
Subjects: Family, Memory, Creative Nonfiction
ISBN   978-0-6488504-3-4 paperback

Hunter Writers Centre
Newcastle NSW 2300
info@hunterwriterscentre.org
hunterwriterscentre.org

Dedicated to the family and friends
who make life memorable

Table of Contents

Memory in Lockdown: Introduction

Alexandra Lewis

'You can't make this stuff up',[1] writes Lee Gutkind, and he is absolutely correct: not only is there an obligation in creative nonfiction to tell the (inevitably subjective) truth, but also – with pleasing frequency – truth can be mighty strange. Who amongst us would have imagined our lives reshaping at speed to meet the global pandemic: the closed borders, the facemasks and elbow bumps, the working and schooling from home (sometimes in pyjamas), the insecurities of employment and health, the families separated on opposite sides of the world?

The writers who have contributed to this volume took part in a workshop course with a twist: we had planned to meet in person, but instead made Zoom our space for interaction and exchange in the latter half of 2020. Across twelve weeks, we got to know each other through our stories. An ever-shifting pattern of tiled faces onscreen. A gallery view of memoirists, travel writers, and personal essayists (and thanks a million, folks, for turning on the camera and smiling!).

This was a novel way of experiencing the intimacy, urgency, and vulnerability of writing the self: a world in which one must click unmute to unmask; where whispered asides around a table migrated to group typed chat; where buffering would more likely refer to issues of internet speed than to a first-time participant shoring themself up for the act of reading aloud and having their words closely, properly, thrillingly, attended to.

---

1   Lee Gutkind, *You Can't Make This Stuff Up* (Boston, MA: Da Capo, 2012).

Central to life writing and the personal essay is, as Phillip Lopate puts it, 'the supposition that there is a certain unity to human experience',[2] and in 2020 we were to an extent (mawkish catchphrase alert) *all in this together* – finding vital commonality not only in the threads of our recollections and observations but also our heightened awareness of renegotiated daily routines. Individuals, families, communities, and nations were (though all inhabiting this same historical pandemic moment) very differently affected by coronavirus. This group of writers cleaved together, finding ways in which technology and narrative could keep us connected in these *unprecedented* times – our *new normal*.

This was creative nonfiction in the age of COVID-19: memory in lockdown.

Memory itself, of course, was not in lockdown. Far from it. Memory and imagination offered a freedom set apart from physical restrictions. As we felt ourselves hampered by unanticipated limitations, creativity burgeoned forth as a kind of escape. Even as supermarket shelves lay bare, the toilet rolls, packets of pasta, and hand sanitisers of the mind were limitless – and these stood only at the point of entry to other, deeper, riches. Reflections on family, on childhood; a serious attention to voice and perspective, structure and risk; bringing the complex contradictions and confusions of identity to life in a way which would arrest or challenge the reader: these were the preoccupations that drew us closer in a time of isolation.

Making use of memory in creativity, while living more remotely than many of us had been accustomed to, no doubt had positive implications for wellbeing. The art of locking down or honing in on memory, in order closely to observe the detail of lived experience, most certainly had positive implications for the pieces of writing offered in this volume.

Some of the pieces deal explicitly with our COVID-19 reality, making knowing reference to the innocence of a before-time, or capturing that feeling of being on the cusp of wide-scale and irrevocable change. For Hannah May in 'Adventure Faces', watching them prepare for the trip of a lifetime, 'there was a childishness about my parents that morning that I hadn't seen for years': bouncing about the house and admiring new hiking equipment, 'we had no idea that COVID-19 would change the world in a few short weeks'. In 'Just Like Him' Ashleigh House's gaze is trained on her mother in the wake of a family death as she sees 'the grief leave her face and migrate down to settle in her hunched shoulders, her shaky hands. COVID-19 meant she couldn't fly back to England [...]. She couldn't hug her mum and cry with her nieces or get drunk on gin with her sister. She was oceans away'. A final goodbye between granddaughter and grandfather is held in an act of shared silent reading over Skype, his local paper accessible on the internet but 'a million miles between us'.

---

2 Phillip Lopate, 'Introduction', *The Art of the Personal Essay* (New York: Anchor, 1995), p. xxiii.

Frankie Miller's 'Summer, 2020' reminds us of that other major recent disaster in our part of the world – the 2019-20 Australian bushfires – as she awakens at a Students of Sustainability conference to find her tent 'covered in ash'. The breeze was 'hot and smoky. It felt bad to be outside'. The orange haze Miller describes creeps and pushes its way into cars and lungs, connecting people 'all across the state' through the constant 'reminder of loss'. Notable is the way this deftly foreshadows the eclipsing event yet to come: 'We had no idea that the fires were only a small taste of how it felt' to inhabit a world in crisis. This compelling piece provides a good example of the way writers in this volume are using voice and pace and expertise (which includes self-knowledge and critical distance) to make concrete detail resonate symbolically without the reader feeling too directed. There is a balance between revelation of emotion or thought and the action of the scene, and my attention is drawn to the small moments, beautifully observed, which illuminate the drama of relationship. Well crafted writing can feel effortless (to read), but to achieve powerful simplicity – 'then I let you go, and you got on the train' – the writer has been working (much like the 'you' to whom this piece is intimately addressed) to 'fold [...] everything away with careful hands'; to pare the writing back in all the right places.

Bleach is topical (and should be only topical in application – we know not to inject it or to drink disinfectant. Right? Despite what certain leaders may tell us?). For a consideration of cleanliness, refuse, respect, and forms of perception and inattention – from a pre-COVID, cleaner's-eye view – look no further than Squidge Lawrence's 'Bleach'. Here is a piece in which every moment earns its place – so many small yet piercing observations knitted together such that not a sentence feels wasted. The unique perspective on – and small interventions in – the worlds of school and courthouse allow for a brilliantly wry tone and pockets of negative space to coalesce: the reader is invited to engage with the fact that 'in the end, we are all just people'. If a vacuum holds the potential to feel like a superhero's jetpack (though more likely than not will, rather, be used to collect indiscriminately the fallen scraps and glittering adornments of life), so too has this persona become 'painfully aware that people who still piss on the toilet seat are making the decisions which affect the rest of people's lives. Accidents happen'.

Our attention to nature has also been refocused, heightened, due to COVID-19. I often note with joy the multi-suburb birdsong permeating Zoom meetings. In Kate Mannell's 'Eucalypts', we see something of the life of trees in connection with our own; we admire the author's awareness of the way a sapling 'grew with me'. Major events and changes (a father's retirement from patrol; barely-mentioned family tensions or 'raised voices'; falling in love and moving in together with a partner) are compressed whereas the sensory detail of trees in the wind or magpies on their branches are given full scope for development. This enhances the lyrical effect of trees as friends (more so than party-going peers at university) and storytellers, and also signals the extended timescale that captivates Mannell's interest: tree time, with a long history of rising and falling.

There is a sustained treatment of 'Lineage' in several pieces, from Charlotte Rae's awareness of 'every lucky star and tennis match, unaccountable decision and unavoidable failure', that led to her place on the family tree; to Lucy Egan's tracing of matrilineal inheritance in 'Herstory'. Egan reports growing up 'on a diet of Mum's family stories', and in a second piece 'Sweet Tooth' we get a proper taste of Egan's recipe for knowing the self through the mixture of ancestral mythology: Barndy's butterscotch pudding! (It is moments like these that I regret the workshops having taken place over Zoom.)

Photographs, as Clarissa Chawner realises in 'Sonder', can be 'overwhelming' – multitudes of rich personal histories displayed 'on every surface' in people's homes – but also provide a useful prompt for breathing imaginative life into our parents' stories, and often thus reframing our own. Rose Lamack's 'Tunnel' unravels a moment of seduction at Masjid Jamek via a later photograph on a train which – laid on the family dining table – gives her mother 'the ghost of a smile' and connects with her father's longings in a different time zone. The matter-of-factness of what is observable and indisputable (times and locations) provides an excellent scaffolding for the tunnelling work of memory done underneath. There is a real intimacy and immediacy in the descriptions of the faces, hopes, and thoughts of both parents. In the smooth melding of what has likely been reported to Lamack of a time before her birth and what is of necessity imagined, embellished, or interpreted, the author is almost absent; and yet, everywhere.

Sandra Joy, affronted by the 'lie' in a 'verbal caption', asks questions about secrecy and belonging in 'Who's The Foreigner?', finding that it is her own mind that is 'punished' by thoughts of her mother's 'adventures of immorality'. Jackson Driver faces head-on the possibility of 'An Unflattering Family Portrait', addressing the audience directly as he ruminates on an image of his 'oh-so chunky' mother ('don't misunderstand me: I'm certainly not being critical'). Weighing difficulty and 'indulgence', this piece allows time to flow forward: 'I wonder too if one day I'll have children of my own, only for them to grow embarrassed and disgusted by whatever substance I'm hooked on twenty years from now'.

An awareness of 'the life that might have been' is central to Charlotte Rae's exploration of work and study options in 'The Academy', as well as the divergent paths that lead Kate Mannell to question where, exactly, is 'Home'? Clarissa Chawner sets out the 'options for people who spend their adolescence growing up in a small town' in her piece 'one plus one equals more', and provides us with a firm sense of place (Newcastle is a 'shock', a 'maze', after 'tight-knit' Walcha). As Mannell writes, those of us with 'wanderlust' who frequently travel to 'gain perspective' might feel thwarted by a 'threatening virus'; reading

'Home', we can relish vicariously escapades ranging from global ('heavy mists, rain, and brief moments of clarity' at Machu Picchu) to local (chanting 'catchy tunes over the loudspeaker to sell roast chickens').

Perhaps the greatest sense of being at home, wherever we are in the world, arises from feeling aware of and reasonably comfortable with one's own (ever-shifting, fluid) identity – in convergence with the genuine acceptance of our self-expression by those around us. Alice Connors in 'Two Attempts' gives us the second ('Did I cry first or Mum?') then the first attempt ('the screaming is infectious') at making her voice heard – 'I think I'm a girl' – and shows the hurt that can ensue when necessary conversations are truncated or avoided. Alice revisits a time when 'I would wear a scarf as a skirt in the mirror, sweating in fear that Mum would come home'; and moves the reader forward to a point where 'I'm going to talk to my therapist about testosterone blockers. I think I'll go onto estrogen eventually, laser off all the hair, get into shape'. A 'third attempt' – a tentative success, though not involving the mother who idolises Chris Hemsworth, and not enumerated in the piece's title – carries concisely the triumph of recognition: 'How are we today, ladies?'

In her excellent edited collection, *Split*, Lee Kofman writes of her frustration with 'the current appetite for a certain type of ending – the redemptive kind'. Happiness and hope have their place (as most certainly they do in *Memory in Lockdown*), but Kofman values equally 'the humility, and realness, of narratives about defeats' – arcs where the 'acquired wisdom is battered, shaky or of the Socrates-kind – "I know that I know nothing"'.[3] Several pieces in the current volume resist easy closure or the sense of having overcome and moved beyond adversity – in many ways, instead, the authors show how past memory and experience envelops our present moment.

The force of the italicised closing apology in Sandra Joy's 'Death Kills' transports the reader to the centre of conscious thought of, we sense, both remembered child and writing adult self; for all of Delia Hoffman's powerful attempts to categorise the partner/carer's experience of terminal illness as a series of notes to self – implying some possibility of order, of learning – we are left in a mood that is 'bare, stark, and lonely': 'I wondered if I was ever going to be warm again'. Through immersion in the mundane minutiae of interactions with customers and machines in 'Responding with a Click', Lucy Neilson Spitzer evokes a lassitude which builds, unbroken, to subsume the question of accomplishment. Hannah McGregor (the talented illustrator of our cover) ends the last of her three short pieces, 'Vehementi', with this violent uncertainty: 'I'm scared of what I will do, what I want to do, and what I should do'. There is, in creative nonfiction, abundant room for tension, for discomfort: honesty is paramount in effective life writing, and growth (or perhaps more simply survival) is so often painful.

---

3   Lee Kofman, 'Introduction', *Split* (Sydney: Ventura, 2019), pp. 15, 17.

No matter your tilt towards hope or defeat, or some vacillation between, there's a grace in the way we as humans craft our stories and strive to make sense of individual and shared experience. This is the 'form, and beat' of Alice Walker's ethos in *Hard Times Require Furious Dancing*.[4] Whether you have been reading and writing your way through this pandemic, or dancing, or even using the lockdown lull to learn a new language or cultivate a sourdough starter (in which case, hats off to you!), be gentle with yourself and appreciate the beauty in the detail. We hope that you enjoy *Memory in Lockdown*.

---

4   Alice Walker, 'Preface: Learning to Dance', *Hard Times Require Furious Dancing* (Novato, CA: New World Library, 2010), p. xvi.

Tunnel

Rose Lamack

It is 8:15pm in Newcastle.

There is something soft in Mum's eyes as I lay the photograph on the dining table. I had rummaged through the stacks of photo albums piled at the back of the garage to find it. Her fingers brush the edge of the photograph and it's almost as if its ink is seeping back into her skin and painting a gallery of good memories before her eyes. The ghost of a smile creeps over her lips. She murmurs something but I don't quite catch it.

It was the first holiday Mum and Dad were going on with no one but themselves – something Mum was rather excited about. They had been married for six months and Mum hadn't really spent any time with Dad at all. In fact, she hardly had space to breathe with his family swarming around them all the time. His sisters, loud and boisterous, would always be making inappropriate comments. His aunties, itching for some drama, always prodded about Dad's past girlfriends. But it was Nana, Mum's fierce and overbearing mother-in-law, whose star quality was the constant provision of unwanted opinions, who irked her the most.

Ah yes, a holiday without the family seemed too good to be true.

She settled into her cushioned seat as the train rattled along. Soon, they would be in Singapore. From there, they would board the cruise and sail onto the ocean beyond. The constant movement was slightly sickening. She was going to be a mother soon. Her belly had already begun to show. It terrified her.

She stared at Dad in that moment, wondering what he would be like as a father. To be quite honest, she didn't really know him. It had only been a year since the first time they'd met.

She smiled to herself as her mind crept back to the tunnel at Masjid Jamek. She had been assigned there to inspect the walls. She'd inched forward, trying to peer closely at a large crack when her foot missed a rung of the ladder and she slipped! Sore and flustered on the ground, her ears perked to the sound of a voice calling out from the darkness. 'Is the floor alright?' it asked. Mum huffed. A silhouette and a set of footsteps neared. Raven black hair, a charismatic smile and a god-awful moustache came into view.

'Reuben,' he said as he extended his hand out to her.

'Malliga,' she said as she took it.

The train jolted and Mum's stomach lurched. She steadied herself, placing her hand on the seat to stop the spinning in her head.

They had bought a camera before their trip away. Dad removed it from a black bag and asked a passenger to snap a picture of them. Huddling together, they smiled. Mum placed her hand on Dad's shoulder and arm, shying away from the camera's click as she hid her body behind his.

'One, two, three!'

The camera clicked with a white flash.

Dad blinked, his eyes clearing. He thanked the passenger as the camera was handed back to him. He had never been one for photos. His sisters always told him he couldn't smile. Alex, his older brother, had the most effortless smile whilst Dad on the other hand, would be caught in a tiresome battle contorting his features in an attempt of one. However, the prospect of adventure was exciting. Exciting enough that it trumped his inability to smile. He didn't hesitate for a moment when he saw the camera on sale.

Mum shuffled around next to him. They would be on the train overnight, and he had decided that they would travel first class (an idea that appealed very much to his wife and not so much to his bank account). He gazed at her for a moment, his wife. It still felt so odd to think that was what she was. Her black hair tumbled upon her shoulders, her eyes twinkled, and her long eyelashes feathered high cheekbones. She was beautiful. It was a wonder he managed to seduce her in that tunnel.

He had worked hard for her. Her father, a devout Hindu, was violently opposed to the idea of a Christian son-in-law. Dad became the primary topic of many village meetings as families gathered together to seek a divine solution to the problem at hand. Mum was threatened to be disowned. This, it seemed, did not deter her. She asserted that she would be with him and him only.

And so, they were wed.

Dad took Mum's hand in his, gently kissing her palm. Soon, he would hold their baby in his arms. He had been waiting so long for a child.

Elsewhere on the train, blankets were being drawn and lights were switching off. Mum nestled her head on Dad's shoulder and their eyes fluttered shut as the train rumbled on to Singapore.

It is 5:15pm in Kuala Lumpur. Dad is finishing a work report.

He sits at his computer, slowly typing away. The tap of the keys is the sound he is most familiar with nowadays. The house no longer echoes with the chatter of his daughters nor their incessant bickering. Instead, it breathes an empty sigh.

He descends the stairs and finds himself in their room. There is nothing in it. Their beds have already been shipped to Australia, along with all their other belongings. He checks the time, wondering what they are doing right now. Is Rose out with her new boyfriend? Is Rayna still practicing her driving?

His wife crosses his mind. Time unravels itself around him and with it, all the years of their marriage. He feels the embers of a warm fondness glow in his chest. He misses her, but knows it is for the best that she is an ocean away. Their children matter the most.

Dad sits back down at his computer again. He types.

The Academy

Charlotte Rae

I knew you'd haunt all of my what-ifs.

I find it remarkable to think how Taylor Swift could have been the veritable poet laureate of my life when I haven't ever been in a single relationship. But the lyrical emotion of her music transcends one single context or story, and her songs have woven around my life and thoughts for eight years now. And so it is, that this line catches in my throat when I sing along – not because I'm thinking of a boy who cheated on me, but of a place – a place that life, or maybe myself, cheated me of.

And it doesn't matter. I don't mind. I'm happy. I have relinquished old dreams. But the truth of it is that I am still haunted by those ghost fantasies, lingering in the corners of my mind, and conjured up by willow trees, polished boots, frosty morning air, gumtrees, piano music, the Canberra skyline, clean-shaven faces, blue eyes, and crisp uniforms.

My eldest brother was seventeen years old when he left home to go to the Australian Defence Force Academy in Canberra, busting to leave this home and town and family and life. We watched him as he was carried away towards our capital in a bus, and Mum cried. He was the first of the four of us to – almost literally – fly the coop, and perhaps the elitist and adventurous path he chose set a high precedent for the rest of us. I was eleven at the time.

My first trip to ADFA was not long after. We all went to his first parade after the notorious 'first six weeks' of military training. It was a six-hour trip from our farm to Canberra, and the only thing I remember about it was our very first stop in Berrima. We went to the park there next to the alpaca farm and Dad cooked sausages while I skipped down to watch the river and Mum huddled away from the wind. How many times since have we repeated the same ritual?

The next day, on the Canberra drive from our motel to the academy, Mum warned the three of us it would be a very boring day but not to complain, because we were there for James's sake. I remember I wore a soft hand-me-down skirt striped in sage and rose hues, but I don't really remember my very first impressions of ADFA. I can imagine though, from all the times I've seen them since, that those impressive gates leading in were the first thing to catch my fancy.

In any case, the thing I do remember vividly is one tiny moment which everything would prove to spring from. I was standing there amid the bright, mid-morning bustle of the Open Day, gazing about at the academy. Lecture halls and climbing walls spread around me and I could see the lush green parade ground from where I stood. And everywhere wandered young men and women with straight backs and a march-like gait, clothed in beautiful khaki and grey or navy-blue uniforms. They seemed full of such direction and vivacity. The 'civilians' – families of the cadets and midshipmen, like us – ambled about in soft clothes and bright colours, all carrying yellow UNSW tote bags inscribed with three words: never stand still.

Those words seemed to string together everything I was seeing. They made sense of the brightness in the cadets' eyes and the spring in the midshipmen's steps. They illuminated why they had all made this terrifying, huge decision, why they chose this path and not a quiet civilian university, why they climbed rock walls and did obstacle courses. I knew right then that I didn't want to stand still either – I wanted to end up here.

That was ten years ago, and I still remember the brightness of the epiphany as it sprung up within me. In any case, there was time yet to think about that. Time yet to decide whether to choose it or my worn-in aspiration of being a literature teacher. So much time: the years between my eleven-year-old self and being 'grown up' spanned before me endlessly. I felt there was a whole life ahead of me before I was James's age.

I don't think I've ever been in any doubt that the appeal started and ended with the academy. Of course, in my enlistment interviews I would say something like, 'I want to join the Defence Force for a chance to serve the nation like so many before …', but I knew it all hung upon ADFA. The seven-year initial minimum period of service – IMPS – for the role I applied for seemed completely worthwhile for the opportunity to study at that university. Four years, after the three at the academy, seemed trifling to be in a job I might not like. And I still think it might have been. Have I not been slogging away these seven years behind a counter at IGA?

But yes, it was ADFA. To me it had taken on some grand mythology: some glistening wonder of adventure, youth, and intelligence. Time after time, I went there for the annual open day, even after James had graduated and our motive switched from supporting him to inspiring me (much to my mother's chagrin) – and I was in love.

It started with Canberra: for as long as I can remember, I've thought it was the most beautiful city – forested, structured, classy. I love that all the streets lead to Parliament House. I love the straight line between that shining white building and the War Memorial. I adore the poplars swaying on the way in, the great dry lake where sheep graze, the circular design, the crisp air, and the military academies. I remember one such open day trip when we drove into the city – through that long stretch with the wind farm to the left – we played *The Man from Snowy River* soundtrack in the car. The glorious nostalgia of those rumbling piano melodies was swept up in the scenery, we were heading towards ADFA, and I knew, I *knew*, this is what I wanted to do. Ever after, when I had doubts, I would play that album. I would shut my eyes and imagine being in an upstairs room at ADFA that overlooked the mountains, listening to that soundtrack as I studied.

To this day, I still maintain it's the most beautiful campus in the world. Everything is both polished and wild. There are poplars, willows, and blossom trees; the buildings are beautiful, and the students dress in crisp uniforms. But it was all part of the mythology I had created of it. I longed to dress in a navy-blue skirt suit and have my hair tied at the nape of my neck. I wanted to be called by my last name and be saluted. I would imagine the look of surprise and awe on townspeople's faces when Mum told them Charlotte had joined the Air Force. I have to confess: I wanted the elitism.

And I wanted the adventure James had found when leaving home. I loved – love – my farm, my home, but I began to see I needed to get away. Truly away, not just to Newcastle where I would still be living with them. It seemed to me that I might never experience anything in life, or grow up, or make my own stories if I did not get far, far away – living on campus at a military university. I imagined the excitement of it all. Perishing mornings on the Parade Ground, feet frozen through leather boots. That inimitable camaraderie with fellow cadets in my house. A blue-eyed boy in uniform kissing me at twilight on that mountain lookout above the city lights.

Did I want a part of the culture of the Defence Force? Perhaps not. Did I want a career there? I don't know. I felt I couldn't know unless I tried. I felt I had to try just for the chance of going there, for experiencing it.
And so, I did.

Sit down and write that letter.
Sign up and join the fight.
Sink into all that matters.
Step out into the light.

It was a lyric I held onto, that year that I went through the enlistment process. Of course, I had my moments of slight pacifist doubt, but that beautiful line of Andrew Peterson's would convince me every time. It tied into 'never stand still' and told me I was doing the right thing.

It was a huge year as ADFA bled into new places in my mind and experience. There was the Defence Recruiting building in Hunter Street – I go past it every week now on my way to Newcastle's inner-city campus, and my stomach lurches in a phantom nervous sensation each time I see it. It's crisp and beautiful in there, full of nervous young teenagers in blazers, and mature officers striding around in uniform. There was the dark room of my medical examination which still haunts me a little with its unnatural discomfort, the bright room where a psychologist cross examined me for an hour, the little room where I had two interviews ending with strong handshakes and encouraging smiles, and the bathroom. I remember it well because of the countless times I frequented it in my nerves. Even now I can remember the potent smell of its tropical hand-soap, and the feeling that surged through me when I went into one of the cubicles after passing my second interview: I shut the door and jumped up and down, whispering *yes, yes, yes!* In that moment, in that cubicle, my entire life expanded around me and before me: not even when I stood on its grounds had I ever felt closer to ADFA.

The academy even found a way to spread into my job at IGA. I vividly remember going to work in that time and feeling like I was living in the past. My shifts felt a little surreal for a while, like they were something that I would leave behind very, very soon. I imagined myself in a new life in six months, six hours away, with that grotty little shop and intimidating bosses and sullen customers mere distant memories of my youth. And I began to feel like I was already living in that memory, working my final shifts.

I'm still there now. The feeling has changed to that of a monotonous nightmare I can't escape.

There are other things that remind me of the enlistment process as well. Around that time, I would often get myself organic peanut butter cups that were ludicrously expensive but divinely good. When I next bit into one, months afterwards, I felt sick with nerves at the very taste: another enlistment ghost. Frozen yoghurt shares a similar fate from the times Dad would drive me to the Marketown Yogurtland after an interview. For a similar reason, I can't imagine ever listening to the *Mamma Mia 2* soundtrack again. The film had just come out at the same time I started the process. I bought the album and would listen to it with Mum or Dad on the car trips to Defence Recruiting and sing every word. We even played it on our way to the airport, to the plane that would take me to Canberra and my final interview – the Officer Selection Board – the day before it was all over.

To this day, and I don't know what this says about my life, I consider it the biggest thing I've ever done: the most new, scary, huge, unprecedented thing that the rest of my life hung upon. My first solo plane trip, wandering around an airport with a boy and a girl I'd just met who had the same destination as me, and the entire terrifying, exciting, surging tumble of events that took place afterwards. That afternoon, the one before my OSB interview, we were given a tour of ADFA: a throng of Army, Navy, and Air Force hopefuls learning about the place we might get to live for three years. I remember the day was overcast

14

and I felt lost. Before dinner in the Mess, we sat upstairs in big leather lounges, giggling with nerves, looking over notes, listening to the group of crass alpha-males shout stories. And I didn't feel like I belonged. I got a creeping feeling in my gut that maybe this would be the atmosphere of life here, and it wasn't for me after all.

But it was the day. The nerves. The weight of the grey sky. And those guys wouldn't have been there: they didn't pass their interviews – either.

The next day I had my interview, first out of my little group of Air Force candidates. The Army and Navy kids went back to ADFA for theirs – there were physical elements involved – but us five, with our sights on blue uniforms, remained at the Ibis hotel.

I still don't really like thinking about my interview. My fingers halt when trying to type about it. I know now all the mistakes I made and the lack of confidence my manner assumed. There was one lady with a kind face, one stern and unyielding, and one man with a smirk. My outfit, a big blue double-breasted jacket, had looked so professional weeks before, but now made me feel uncomfortably masculine and unlike myself. I didn't go up to shake their hands afterwards – their table seemed so high up and far away – but I think I'll regret it until my dying day.

After the interview, the kind-faced officer led me along a path and into the hotel's foyer where she left me. I sat on a high stool looking out at the dove-grey sky that weighed down upon the morning and my spirit. I clasped my hands and tried not to think. When she returned, she sat across from me near a fire and said the words, 'Unfortunately we've decided...'

Everything I'd aspired for crashed around me in torrents. I couldn't comprehend how she had said those words, how this could be the ending. And yet a feeling crept in that told me it was always going to end like this. No sooner had she said the words than I felt I had heard them a million times and they were old and worn out.

I needed a bit more assertiveness. They felt I didn't have the leadership qualities yet. I could come back in a year, and she hoped I would.

I didn't. I couldn't.

I could spend reams on the following twenty-four hours. I could describe the room I spent the day in as boy after girl joined me from their interviews with tears or jubilant smiles. We played Monopoly, and I beat all those obnoxious seventeen-year-old boys, and I still consider that the grand success of the week. That night I went to ADFA for the last time, and ate in the Mess again. I haven't seen it since. At that time, I still thought I might return, but when the time came around the next year, I spent one trembling evening wrestling with myself. I knew that what I had chased after all those years was a fantasy, and not the reality of being an officer in the Air Force. So, I settled in for the second semester of my first year of Law, and haven't looked back since.

Well, almost.

I remember a time I was walking through the Callaghan campus to go to class. It was spring: the new day was fresh and cool. The damp, early morning air was fragrant with eucalyptus. My leather boots crunched on the pavement beneath me. It felt like an exquisite moment in time – like I was so alive and in the prime of my life.

But a tugging sadness filled my spirit as I looked up at the gumtrees. My thoughts were pulled to another university bordered with eucalypts, where the air was fresher, the grounds clearer. Where there were blossom trees blooming in corners, and the people walking past me wore shades of blue and green, and strode in a steady march with straight shoulders and bright eyes. And I knew right then that, as long as I lived, as happy as I become, I would be haunted by ghost fantasies of the life that might have been.

one plus two equals more

Clarissa Chawner

It's my opinion that there are only two options for people who spend their adolescence growing up in a small town.

Option one: despise the small town, move away as soon as the opportunity presents itself and never return, apart from the occasional visit.

Option two: become attached to the small town and never leave, live there forever, having multiple generations of children and grandchildren.

I don't look down on anyone who does option two, but I couldn't think of anything worse.

In 2006, my father got a new job. As a family, we – my father, my mother, my brother and I – moved approximately 394 kilometres across the state. From Lismore, a bustling city filled with roughly 28,000 people, to the small town of Walcha. Population: 1,451.

It was a shock.

I don't really remember living in Lismore. I have vague memories of walking to school, but catching the bus home. Going to the markets with my parents, in the carpark of Lismore Square.

One of the two things I do remember clearly is that, on Saturdays, my brother and I would go to our grandparents' house. I saw this as a wonderful day filled with games of tennis and crossword puzzles; watching *Chicken Run*; and, of course, an endless supply of scotch finger biscuits slathered in butter.

On summer evenings, before Mum and Dad came to pick us up, Grandma would let Murdoc and I water the garden with her. We would take turns holding the hose, spraying the colourful array of flowers, then eventually spraying each other.

I was fascinated by the laundry chute that connected the upstairs and downstairs parts of the house. Mesmerised, I would watch dirty clothes slide *down* the chute and magically disappear around the bend. Racing downstairs, I would discover that, like every other time, the clothes had landed in the waiting basket. The laundry chute also puzzled me. It was an easy way to get the washing downstairs.

What was the easy way to get the washing upstairs?

Once, I tried to convince Grandma that I would fit down the laundry chute. She wouldn't let me try.

The other thing I remember clearly is the trips to the beach. Almost every weekend during summer, Mum and Dad would pack us all up into the old silver Camry we used to have, and drive the half-hour trip from Lismore to Ballina.

I would always get a thrill when the ocean was finally visible on the horizon.

Mum had packing for the beach down to a fine art. Everyone had swimmers, shoes and hats. Mum had a fold-up chair to sit on, and an umbrella to sit under. The esky was full of snacks – chicken and cheese sandwiches safely encased in zip-lock bags, cut up watermelon and sliced oranges, and a few sneaky chocolates.

No one was allowed to swim until they had put sunscreen on.

The routine began with swim in the morning, then a break for morning tea. Then more swimming, followed by fish and chips from the takeaway shop. The afternoon was spent collecting shells and constructing sandcastles. Dad and Murdoc would pick a random spot in the sand and just dig, until water began to appear at the bottom, and the hole was so deep that they could both fit inside.

Before we left, we were allowed to get an ice cream for the drive home to distract from the uncomfortable feeling of being wet and sandy.

Every trip to the beach was the same. It never grew old.

I have many memories of Walcha. I spent eleven years of my life living there.

It's not a big place.

The town is divided into quarters by the two main streets, each quarter named after a direction on the compass. I've lived in the northern and western parts of town, and my parents now own a house in the western section. When they bought the house, it needed a new roof, a fresh coat of paint, and a major garden overhaul.

They've been there for two years now.

The inside of the house is now a pristine white rather than off-green, and Mum has ripped out all the rose bushes. She sold them for fifteen bucks a pop; never one to miss an opportunity. They've now been replaced with rows of lavender bushes. Out the back, there is a line of raised garden beds, overflowing with kale, cauliflower and corn. Our beloved dog is buried by the shed, succulents slowly taking over the bare patch of dirt that was her favourite spot.

Despite all of this, that house is not my home. I've never lived there. When I come to visit, I sleep in the spare room.

The cottage we lived at in the northern section of town is just a pale fragment of memory. It was small. Very small. Mum attempted to grow rosemary, but I think it died.

It's the house in the western part of Walcha that is the cherished one. With its olive-green roof, glassed-in verandah, it sits regally on its double block of land on the hill. The house was extremely old. The colour of the paint was different in every room: an awful goldfish-yellow in the bedrooms, blue in the kitchen, and white in the lounge room. The bathroom and dining room were add-ons of plain brick. The wooden boards that made up the ceiling were spaced so far apart that bugs were prone to falling through.

As children, Murdoc and I spent many afternoons in the backyard.

It was *vast*.

The lower level was where Mum cultivated her multitudes of fruits and vegetables. Tomatoes, spring onions, garlic, chillies, and every herb under the sun. Strawberries ran wild in the garden bed on the far wall, runners overtaking more and more of the garden each year. In spring and summer, ripe strawberries were fair game. If we didn't pick them soon enough, they were ant food – or dog food, until she decided the blood and bone fertiliser tasted better.

A set of curving wooden steps took you up to the middle level. Whoever built the deck up there did a masterful job. It even had a bridge. In the height of summer, the overhanging wisteria vines provided the perfect amount of shade for evening dinners. When the weather was warm, Murdoc and I would put up the hammocks and laze around, throwing wisteria flowers at one another until we got thirsty in the heat.

The black compost bin stood like a lone soldier on the upper level, surveying the empty block at the back of the house. The grass turned out to be mostly dandelions, much to Dad's disgust.

Honestly, the town itself is actually quite pleasant. Unassuming. Two grocers, two cafes, three pubs. A few other miscellaneous shops. Everything shut at six p.m., except for the service station. That shut at eight. The river curved through the middle of town, narrow enough that in some parts you could jump across. Sculptures donated by local artists dotted the levee banks. Walcha was very proud of its art presence.

All the kids in town attended Walcha Central during primary school. Student numbers diminished in high school, though. The kids whose families had lived here for more than three generations were shipped off to boarding school in Armidale or Tamworth. If the family had big money, they went to Sydney. Something about a private school education being *better*.

The dregs attended Walcha Central for high school. The teachers did their best; they had to be thick-skinned to survive. The government doesn't like to send its precious education funding to the country.

I went to Walcha Central.

I think I turned out fine.

While Walcha itself isn't too bad, it's the people that live there who really bother me. The phrase *tight-knit community* is code for *everyone knows your business before you do.* Everyone knows your name, your parents' names, where you live, what your job is, what you ate for breakfast, and so on. You can't go down the road to buy a loaf of bread without running into someone you know. Then you have to say hello and make polite small talk.

Everyone knows everyone, and there's a good chance they're related somehow. It's so incestuous, it's disturbing.

The attitudes of the people are just suffocating. Just because you own some dry farmland and a few cattle, doesn't mean you're better than anyone else.

In 2017, I moved to Newcastle.

Population: 450,000.

It was, once again, a shock.

The traffic astounded me more than anything. Cars everywhere, on all these multi-lane roads and multi-lane roundabouts! I'd never had to merge lanes before in my life. Walcha didn't even have traffic lights! The phrase *peak hour traffic* took on a whole new meaning. I didn't drive anywhere when school children were being picked up or dropped off, or when people were commuting home from work at the end of the day. Too many cars. The city felt like a labyrinth; Google maps was constantly open on my phone because I had no idea where I was going. My woeful sense of direction was constantly confused.

And the people.

All the people.

Everywhere.

I quickly learned to not go grocery shopping on weekends. People didn't look where they pushed their trolleys. It was like a bizarre parody of the cars on the road – trolleys trying to merge in front of other trolleys, dirty looks a substitute for honking your horn.

Once, in my first few months of living in Newcastle, I made the mistake of going to Westfield at Kotara, on one of the days leading up to Christmas. After I found a park, I had to navigate the shopping centre.

It was a maze. The crowds were endless.

I think I lasted all of twenty minutes before I attempted to find my car again, which took another twenty minutes. On the way home, when I took a wrong turn, I had to pull over so I could cry.

But this was my chance at anonymity. Sweet, sweet anonymity.

No one in Newcastle knew who I was. They didn't know my parents' names, where I lived, what I did for a job, or what I ate for breakfast.

It was amazing.

I've lived in four places during the three years I've lived in Newcastle. I wouldn't call them *homes*, either.

The first one was a cockroach-riddled unit three blocks from the beach. The rent was expensive, for the poky little kitchen, and a bathroom that looked like it had been vomited straight from the sixties. The only place to do washing was the ancient, coin-operated washing machine in the communal laundry downstairs. It was three dollars per wash, and would only accept one-dollar coins. During summer, the salt breeze coming from the coast was scorching. Night-time provided no relief, only more noise from the street.

But with my rose-tinted glasses on, it was perfect.

I went through a succession of roommates before the apartment was sold.

After that was a lovely two-storey townhouse. Rent was more expensive, but this place had under-cover parking. It had a huge kitchen with a glass cooktop. It had a laundry! I quickly had to invest in a washing machine. While there was roughly the same number of cockroaches, the street was much quieter.

I felt as though I was moving up in the world.

And then I came plummeting *down*.

My roommate at the lovely townhouse did a runner to live in an actual house, with a yard for his dogs. I scrambled to find someone to replace him.

After two long months of my parents generously paying the other half of my rent, I resigned myself to the fact that I would have to move out. An acquaintance from university told me she had a spare room, and she and her roommate were looking for a third person.

What I thought was a timely blessing was, in fact, one of the most regrettable decisions of my life.

The house was *disgusting*.

Aside from being poorly renovated by someone who didn't know how to lay electrical wiring properly, the walls were paper-thin – privacy soon became a foreign concept. It retained heat in summer and was freezing in winter. The bedrooms and bathroom had a mould problem. Black spots bloomed abundantly on the ceilings.

But what made the place really vile was that no one knew how to clean. Before I moved in, the girls didn't have a vacuum, or a toilet brush. No *toilet brush*.

After many petty arguments, the two girls moved out and two equally petty girls replaced them. Between the two of them, these girls owned three cats, yet neither of them seemed to understand how often a cat litter tray needed to be emptied.

I quickly grew tired of cleaning.

I slept at my partner's more than I slept in my own bed.

I firmly believe that house was cursed to bring out the worst in people, myself included.

Then finally, there was a light at the end of the tunnel. After many tears and much stress-induced hair loss, I moved out, and moved in with the aforementioned partner. We now live in a peaceful little apartment, just the two of us. Everything is clean and quiet. I don't find stray cat hairs in my food.

It's bliss.

Despite taking option one and embarking on this tumultuous housing journey, I find myself unable to escape my roots.

They are too deep.

At every house I've lived, I found myself attempting to cultivate a garden. Growing plants in pots is very different to growing them in the ground, I've discovered.

First, it was lovely ferns and lilies. When they inevitably died, I hastily purchased replacements from Bunnings. When the replacements died, I decided that maybe temperamental plants were not within my limited skillset.

In the horror-house, I had a garden of herbs – also in pots – hidden out the back, away from the cigarette smoke of the other girls. They didn't do well there; not enough sun. Nothing did well in that house.

But now I have a courtyard. I still can't plant things in the ground, but I do have space for bigger pots. I have the few herbs that did survive sequestered in the kitchen, while I try to build my own private jungle outside.

It's a work in progress.

I have sunflowers, beans, tulips, lettuce, spring onions, and many, many succulents. The tomato plants sadly died.

There's always going to be some losses.

When I repot plants, I always wear gardening gloves and a wide-brimmed straw hat. My partner tells me I look like a farmer. I'm always equal parts offended and pleased.

I visit the beaches in Newcastle often – or at least, whenever I have the time. In winter, it's for a walk along the shore, to feel the icy chill of the water and the sand under my toenails. I'm drawn to the sound of the waves, the constant roar as they break and recede, the salty tang of the ever-present sea breeze.

In summer, I swim. I find a sense of relief, floating in the waves. When I stagger out – it's always ungainly – I feel *cleansed*.

Afterwards, I seem to find myself pulling into a drive-thru. My order is the same: large fries and a soft-serve cone.

I crave the salty taste of the chips after a good swim, chased by the sweetness of the ice cream. It distracts from the feeling of being sandy on the drive home.

Maybe, there are new options in adulthood.

Just Like Him

Ashleigh House

It was nine months ago today that my mother came into my bedroom, eyes red and puffy, face drawn, to tell me that her father had passed away.

In the moments before this, I had woken up to the sound of voices, muffled through my bedroom door. I remember feeling irritated that I was forced to be conscious so early on my one day off. What could have possibly been so pressing that my family needed to discuss it at seven a.m.? On a Friday! Everything had been fine last night, ordinary.

It wasn't long until I found out.

As my mother sat down heavily on my bed, devastation dulled her usually bright face. I could see my brother in the hallway, a mess of confusion and shock, slumped on the floor. Then my mum was crying, and my brother was crying, and I think I was crying too. While I had been lamenting a few hours of lost sleep, my mother's whole world had changed. She was without a dad. Her mother without a husband. Grandchildren without a grandfather.

In the days that followed, I saw the grief leave her face and migrate down to settle in her hunched shoulders, her shaky hands. COVID-19 meant she couldn't fly back to England, where he lived with the rest of our family. She couldn't hug her mum and cry with her nieces or get drunk on gin with her sister. She was oceans away. Helpless. Directionless. Left alone to drown in her grief.

I wouldn't have blamed her for falling apart at this point. While he regularly annoys me to no end, the idea of being without my own dad makes my chest hurt. Like someone has reached in and squeezed my heart tight. My mother is a dad's girl through and through. As a kid, she spent her days after school sitting on her front wall, waiting for him to come home and carry her to the house on his shoulders. She happily spent her weekends with him, while her siblings were out causing trouble. Even when my dad came along, my grandad was her number one.

I waited on tenterhooks for the inevitable explosion, to see her grief swallow her up. But it never did. Within a few days, she was back to cooking and cleaning, and doing her paperwork. Grief ached dull in my chest as I approached Mum ironing one day, her potential breakdown looming heavy in the house. Her hands gripped the iron tight, smoothing a shirt with meticulous precision.

'You can leave that, you know. I'll do it,' I had said to her.

'That's alright, it keeps me busy. I can't just sit around and mope. What good will that do?' Her voice was resolute. Her eyes never left the shirt. It occurred to me then that a breakdown was not inevitable at all. It was never going to happen. She would be sad, have her bad days, and miss him deeply – but her strength was enduring. It was the same silent, resilient strength my grandad had. Evident as he battled emphysema for years, then lung cancer in his final months. When he watched his home burn down as a kid. When he stood supportive as my mum left for a better life in Australia. Helping her to pack, pulling together the documents, and driving her to the airport. A selfless act that I imagine must have torn him apart.

Putting others before himself was second nature, and it is to my mum as well. It's a trait I admit to lacking and something I've always felt envious of. My younger brother has it. That nurturing, deeply empathetic disposition. It radiates from him, in his gentle smile and soft touch, just like Mum and Grandad. It draws people in. When my granddad passed and my aunt posted the news to Facebook, her feed was full of praise for him. Comment after comment lauding him for being a good man. Decent and kind. It's the same praise my mum receives for being a loving, devoted nurse. The same comments my brother gets on school reports, 'so unusually soft and caring for a teenage boy'. It's such a deeply admirable, beautiful trait. I remember the last time we went to England on holiday and the three of them – my grandad, my brother, and my mum – sat eating breakfast together. I paused in the threshold of the dining room and watched as they shared smiles and soft laughter. I felt my heart break a little. Their inherent goodness was overwhelming. Just three decent people that deserved the world.

What my grandad did pass to me was a quiet, contemplative nature. On our last Skype call together we sat, a million miles between us, and read his local newspaper. His, a physical copy, mine on the internet. It was simple. Very few words spoken. As we read, I could hear his breath battle through his body, clawing to get out with every exhalation. But he didn't complain. He asked me how I was, and I asked him too. He said, 'still here' and that was that. We didn't need to talk about what we were reading or share our thoughts, wax poetic about the weather or moan about our aches and pains. The silence was comfortable and simply us. When we finished, we said goodbye. He died three hours later.

It was just two days ago that my mother opened her birthday card from her parents. For the first time in forty-nine years, it was signed *Love, Mum*. No dad. She held the card in shaky hands, and I watched as she felt the fist of grief punch her in the gut. Her face started to crumple; her body closing in on itself. But in the next blink, her sadness had been contained, and she stood tall and strong again. Resilient, just like always. Just like him.

Bleach

Squidge Lawrence

STAGE I

Among the many pointless and insipid questions we ask children, one of the most common is, 'If you had a superpower, what would it be?' When faced with this question, my immediate and unwavering answer was always, 'flying', and was shocked when my friends, who purported to have good judgement, chose to be invisible.

Adults, on the rare occasion where this question is asked during icebreakers, have arrived at the general consensus that teleportation is the best answer.

'Think of how much time you spend driving places,' they say.

My answer is still, of course, flying. It has become a peculiar source of pride that I have not compromised on my superpower integrity. I am not one of those superpower-for-convenience types. I like to think that the people who chose invisibility and teleportation were nosey as children and impatient as adults.

The irony of this is that, not only am I a bad flyer, I now work in the industry of being invisible. It is one of the only upsides to being a cleaner. Conversations that would usually turn to whispers when others pass within earshot, continue as if I am merely part of the furniture.

'Felix, you can't be chasing the girls around,' one of the teachers says. 'You're too young to have a girlfriend.' In the next room over, one of the staff members is on the phone to a parent. 'He's ripped out all the plants again.' And in the office, 'Jackson's had an accident and we've run out of spare shorts. Would you be able to come and pick him up?'

Of course, it is not just during conversations that people forget you are there. Notes scribbled on post-its, bookmarked self-help books on desks, and letters of notice, all lie absentmindedly on people's desks. Courthouses are serial offenders for leaving sensitive information about the place. Tuesday is sexual offences day, and it is the busiest day of the week by far. Mounds of files, with names and charges in block letters on the front, sprawled across the floors and desks of judges' offices. There is one desk that always heaps their sex-with-a-minor cases in front of their phone. I wish they would put it somewhere else, so I don't have to contort my arm when I'm trying to wipe everything down.

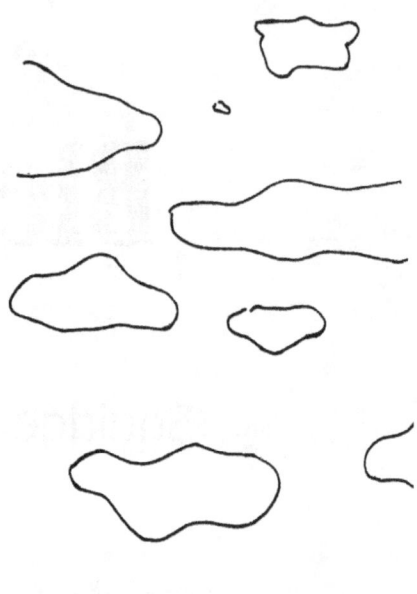

'There's a big case coming up tomorrow,' Chris from level 1 says. 'Keep your eye on that one.'

By far the most sensitive piece of information I have learnt during my time there is that judges have fake spiders on their walls, and treadmills squeezed into their offices. One had a smashed porcelain head which was presumably once used to hold their wig. A tragic demise that had absolutely nothing to do with the cleaners, and certainly could not have been done while dusting the countertop. I have become painfully aware that people who still piss on the toilet seat are making the decisions which affect the rest of peoples' lives. Accidents happen.

But empty offices tell sweet stories too. A sign on the wall over a bunch of printer cords ripped from their nesting says, 'GOODBYE OUR DEAR FRIEND. YOU WILL BE MISSED.' On desks, there are photos of family holidays and pets, awards, and children's drawings.

GOODBYE OUR DEAR FRIEND
YOU WILL BE MISSED
RIP

DIL - AP - I - DA - TED (adjective)

in a state of disrepair or ruin
as a result of age or neglect

STAGE II

In the staff room, a teacher's aide approaches me while I am wiping the tables. We have previously exchanged half-smiles as we pass each other in the walkways. She potters about in the kitchen for a minute or two, looking for something to do with her hands while I wait for the incoming question.

'Do you work here full-time?' she finally asks. I am impressed by her diplomacy. These lines of questioning always have the same conclusion but arrive there via wildly different techniques. Some go for the abrupt, others for the work around, some have such an awkward time they give up before they get the answer they are looking for.

I decide I like her.

'I'm a student,' I say. 'Arts with English. Not that I don't love wiping tables for seven hours a day, of course,' I add. We talk for a little while longer. I convince myself that, if I asked her what superpower she would have, it would be flying.

At one-thirty, I see Angus waving from the end of the playground. I put my bucket down while he wanders over. He never rushes anywhere. The patterned sleeves of our uniforms look like matching tattoos until almost the last second.

'Bloody hell, someone needs to tell these kids to eat some fibre. I swear to god every afternoon that back toilet is blocked.'

'I'll leave that one to you, then,' I say.

'I'm trying to work out who it is,' he says. 'I've got it down to a few it might be, I reckon.'

'What a fun game.'

I can never tell whether his toothless grin is because he thinks what I've said is funny, or whether he's just laughing at me.

The principal seems to always find these moments to walk past. I have never seen him smile or frown and so I imagine a look of disappointment onto his face that we are standing around having a chat. The look suits him, I think. I'm sure the constant stoic expression is the cause of his unwrinkled skin, but young skin on old men makes them look miserable.

Angus and I split up, not wanting to antagonise the enemy. I work through the multi-storey, listening to the snippets of classes as I pass them by – multiplication, continents, what to do if an adult touches you. In the sideroom where students are brought out for extra help, a whiteboard says:

'CHLOE NEEDS TO PRACTICE DILAPIDATED'

Why do people always write these notes in capital letters?

STAGE III

From time to time, a student will make a runaway attempt. They usually head up to the top gates, or behind the basketball courts. This time, we look at each other for a moment before making a value judgement. The boy stays where he is.

Around the next corner, a teacher is walking around the playground.
'Has anyone been past here?'
'I haven't really been paying attention, sorry,' I say. She walks off.

At the same place on a different day, a boy sees me and jumps back around the corner. Rude. When I enter the building, I see a group of teachers standing in a doorframe, pointing in a variety of directions, debating strategy.
'Are you missing someone?' I ask.
'Err, yeah,' he says, off-kilter.
'There was a boy with red hair around the side of the building,' I say, and they peel off in the direction of the sighting.

It has become somewhat of a game to me, picking enemies and allies. At first, I thought I was just making a spur-of-the-moment decision based on how I was feeling. But after a few incidents, a pattern began to emerge. If they look me in the eyes and keep doing what they want, we are allies. It is us versus them, and we are a team. I thought it was because I was impressed by their hostile confidence when they looked me dead in the eyes and then bet on the fact that I wouldn't challenge them. It felt only right to make good this judgement.

But the more it happens, the more I think that it is because I am upset at the others for hiding. It is as though they are saying 'you are one of them' – one of the adults that make their lives miserable and who hand out arbitrary punishments because they like the feeling of being in control. And so, just like with the other runaways, I do what they expect of me.

STAGE IV

In the staff room, the teachers who I have dubbed the 'two satans of the two-storey' wipe down tables with kitchen towel.

'I wonder when the last time these were cleaned,' one of them muses to the other, loudly.

'I don't think they've been wiped all year,' the other exclaims, several decibels above that of a usual discussion between friends.

For the sake of my sanity and their wellbeing, I ignore them, continuing to my cleaning cupboard on the other side of the room.

'Oh, she had her earphones in! Not hearing a word we're saying,' one says. I turn the tap on all the way, letting the violent spray of water drum out the incessant chitter. When my bucket is full, I brush past them, sending a look over my shoulder as I walk out the door. I do not decry people who enjoy spending time around children but, just because you spend most of your time in a primary school, does not mean that you are required to act like a child yourself. I resist the temptation to ask the blonde woman how her divorce is going.

I spend most of my day listening to students complain about their teachers and teachers complain about their students, but they spend so long together that, if one group wasn't so short and high-pitched, you'd barely be able to tell the difference between the two. If the 'two-storey satans' have a problem, maybe they should talk to me about it.

Because of this, it is very difficult to pick a permanent side in the ongoing student-teacher battle. It's like sport, watching them play each other, appreciating ruthless takedowns, but not wanting to get too invested in the rows of people running head-first into each other over and over again.

The only team here that has my loyal support is the General Assistant. He rolls his eyes at the teachers (but only a little bit) and he acts as though the students do not exist. On hot days, when the staffroom is unoccupied, we silently stand in the stream of cold air coming from the air-con.

In one of the smaller rooms next to the two-storey, the whiteboard still says:

'CHLOE NEEDS TO PRACTICE DILAPIDATED'

But Chloe really does not need to practice dilapidated. After all, the teacher in 5/6C pronounced 'debris' wrong yesterday. Why do some people get to decide what's worth knowing?

STAGE V

When I ask Angus what he would
do if he won the lottery, he says,
    'Probably just the morning shift.'

If the judge with the porcelain head had
to choose a superpower, I bet it would
be teleportation.

STAGE VI

I zone out for the second consecutive hour. Planning essays, to-do lists, working
out what I need to find in the way of Christmas presents.

I shoulder the vacuum, strapping it across my chest and velcro it around my waist.
It feels like a jetpack, ready to propel me into the sky. But instead of pushing
me up and away, it suctions onto the floor and slurps around, collecting scraps
of torn paper and grass from people's boots. Occasionally, I see something glint
in the light. Maybe it's a paperclip, maybe it's someone's lost earring. I vacuum
it up without checking.

As per the Australian legal procedure, to be guilty of a crime, the accused must
be proven to have mens rea. In most cases, where the accused does not have
actual knowledge of the material facts, they cannot be found guilty of the crime
of which they are accused.

The jury rooms are a mess. The recycling bins are full of rubbish. I stand there, looking at the two bins side by side.

Recycling – Rubbish.
Recycling – Rubbish.

The bins have clear instructions. The packaging has clear instructions. There were two options. I would have hoped that a group of people who have been tasked with making a decision between guilty and not guilty would know how to correctly sort their rubbish. Errors on one front cost me a few minutes of swearing and rummaging, the other costs someone a jail sentence. I send a prayer for whoever's fate is being decided.

In the downstairs offices, the floor is caked with staples, and there is a full take-away cup upside down in the bin. The next day, they complain that the carpet smells like coffee.

STAGE VII

At 12:25 I sit on the concrete behind the hall to eat my vegemite sandwich. Despite being right next to the disabled toilets, it is the best spot in the school. Occasionally, this is ruined when the GA uses the toilets for a secret shit but, for the most part, the only interruption is the gentle hum of the traffic. No screaming pre-schoolers or hoarse teacher's aides. On the oval, a solitary cockatoo patrols the muddy ground for his lunch, and by his oversized waddle, he is quite good at it. Gum trees and the occasional bottlebrush dust the perimeter, and the spout of the factory puffs steam into the air from between the fork in a tree. If you are not paying close attention, it looks as the though the tree is on fire. But unlike smoke, the vapour quickly disappears into the atmosphere, as if it was never there.

STAGE VIII

In the end, we are all just people. It is not us versus them – kids versus adults, judges versus the accused. Despite what every police show and news story tries to make you believe, it is not even guilty versus innocent. It is merely guilty versus not enough evidence.

Angus still hasn't won the lottery, but he was talking about quitting and getting a job at the servo. He hasn't been at work for three weeks.

People are allowed to choose teleportation if they want to. Not everyone who doesn't want to fly is wrong. Maybe they are just afraid of heights.

Eucalypts

Kate Mannell

There are roughly nine hundred species of eucalypt identified in Australia, so far. Only in the last couple of years has my interest in these trees really developed. I've lived with the eucalypts all my life. I'm only just getting to know them now.

It started before I was born, when my parents stood in the shade of a eucalyptus tree on the property where our lives would unfold for the next twenty years. It was a place where the grass would remain lush and cool when the summer sun blistered the arboreal top storey. The highway was far enough away that the only sounds were whispers of wind or the hesitant shrilling of insects. Open patches of eucalypt forest still clustered on the hills, but now grazing land dominated the area. The trees that had spent thousands of years rising and falling like the tides now only fell. Most new saplings were crushed by hard-hooved animals or cleared for new houses.

My parents arrived shortly after the shining fences and fresh, sandy-coloured timber posts had sectioned off the land. Youth radiated from their features, bright skin, and genuine smiles. They were happy as they sat on a worn picnic blanket in the tall grass, sipping from chalking plastic champagne flutes in the mid-autumn warmth.

Less than a dozen trees remained on our block by the time black plastic and rusted reo mesh were laid out and ready for the pouring of the first slab. A timber frame morphed into a solid structure of bricks, coated in clay-coloured cement render. At the end of the steep driveway of loose russet dirt, the aluminium roof glistened in the sunlight.

Once I was old enough to understand, my father would tell of how he noticed a small sapling in the grass while he was mowing. Saved from the equalising blades, it grew with me. Its long lanceolate leaves would create rippling mirages of shadow and light against the house. After a storm, long strips of bark would be splayed across the yard, revealing bare sections of white and burgundy characteristic of ribbon gum.

A little brother followed. I was thrown over the fence to the neighbour as my parents raced off towards the hospital. They only made it a kilometre down the road. A scraggly eucalypt marks the place on the side of the road where my brother entered the world.

School began and I saw my first fairy. Kicking over a bright red toadstool behind the office building, a small figure in orange drifted up past me towards the overhead tree branches. My mother told me the hollows in the eucalypts were fairy homes, prompting me to leave small tokens in the aged crevices.

The wheels of the patrol car crunched down the driveway a final time. The high-speed chases, flashing lights and mangled bodies had taken a toll on my father. He retreated, a haunted shell of his former self.

The wilds beyond the back fence beckoned me from sight of the house as I evaded raised parental voices. Dancing through nettles and blackberries, I walked the tightrope of a fallen eucalypt until the light faded and hunger drove me back home.

It was still and grey the afternoon I left, passing under trees exhausted by a turbulent summer. My high school sentence had been served so I escaped to another land. Tropical wetlands, desolate steppes, rocky lake districts, Andean altiplanos, cloud forests and Amazonian jungles all dazzled me, but something was missing. My desperation to be free was tempered by the awful feeling of plummeting into something I wasn't ready for. I ached for the home I had left.

Parked at a dusty inland petrol station on a quiet highway in Argentina, I found myself standing in the shade of a tree. Its long, curved leaves danced in the wind just above my head. Reaching up, I plucked one from its stem and crushed it in my hand. The sweet oil, scented of pine and mint, washed through me and tugged at my chest.

Outside the window of my small apartment on the university campus back in Australia, a tall eucalypt kept me company as I struggled to make connections with the party-people living in the building. The fire alarm went off frequently in the early hours, drunken students leaving noodles on the stove too long or forgetting to crack a window during their sessions. The branches of the eucalypt seemed within jumping distance from the ledge under my window, so I decided if there really was a fire, that was my escape plan.

Storms of torrential rain and flashing light would rouse me from sleep, and I'd watch helplessly as the tree outside fought against wild winds. The next morning, magpies would hop along its sturdy branches, gurgling their song into the morning stillness.

Before my first year of study was done, I fell in love. Another year after that, we had settled into a small suburban home together. Beyond the back fence, multicoloured lorikeets squealed in the proud Angophoras trees, a genus of Eucalypt, whose distinctive trunks are patched in the colours of rain clouds and far western dirt. Standing in the morning shadows of those trees, the chore of the washing felt more like a pastime.

We recently went on a road trip out to the south western part of the state. The Australian Inland Botanic Gardens at Mildura boasts a Mallee estimated to be over two thousand years old. It was hard to believe that the unassuming plant, bulbous at its base with sparsely vegetated, gnarled branches, had existed for so long. I wondered what stories had occurred on the red dirt and sage-coloured scrub beneath its leaves.

The place I grew up was our final stop on the trip. The land welcomed me home, rolling hills and grassy paddocks with their eucalypt patches filling me with peace. Tension suffocated the house; the remaining inhabitants almost unrecognisable. Outside nothing had changed, though I was seeing with new eyes.

There are at least three different eucalypt species I now recognised on the block. *Eucalpytus rubida* surveys the valley, reaching for the stars after nightfall. I admire the height and grace the twenty-two-year-old tree has accomplished and wonder if it feels the same toward me. *Eucalyptus melliodora* provides shade for the remaining patches of thick grass while the hollows in the rough bark of *Eucalyptus bridgesiana* grow wider with time.

My life has developed among the eucalypts, yet it is only now I really see them. It is reassuring to know there are more species out there for me to learn with and live with. Trees can live for hundreds of years, and there is an untold future to take place in the shade of their leaves.

Note to Self

Delia Hoffman

Note to Self: That TV commercial is trying to sell you something, not make you miserable.

Just saying, you idiot. It's insurance for the over 55s, not your lost future life.

Note to Self: Remember who, and how, you say 'you're wrong' to.

After many months seeing many specialists who were unable to find the source of Brian's discomfort, the result came from the oncologist. 'Brian, you have pancreatic cancer. The tumour is in a very difficult place. Removal is almost impossible. Most patients have only between six months and a year ... you need to make plans ...'

I can't remember the rest. I do remember my response: No, no, you're wrong. This is not possible. We have teenagers. Try again. Pancreatic cancer? Fuck no. Wrong answer. I'd forgotten who I was speaking with. The professionals have the training. They will be right.

Advice comes out of the woodwork when there is a cancer diagnosis. It comes from people with no qualifications. Like borers undermining solid framework of medical research, it can debilitate your resolve. We had suggestions of heat treatment. Alkaline treatment. Almond kernel treatment. Exotic mushroom treatment. Eat/drink organic. Eat less. Eat more. Go lactose free. Give up white poison. Which one – Salt? Sugar? Refined flour? Suggestions of mindfulness remedies, yogic chants, and hypnosis. Pray.

We both wanted to say, you're wrong and fuck off with your quackery. It would, however, have ruined excellent friendships and had cataclysmic family ramifications. I'd be the one left to deal with the fallout.

Not all those with a terminal illness will welcome your suggestions. Allow them to say, no thanks. I found it very difficult to tell anyone, close to us or not, that Brian was not looking for unconventional treatments. His cancer is specific to him. Your stories of success are specific to that patient. So please understand why we're not interested in your suggestions.

It is so hard to see someone you love suffering. Friends, to be helpful, be considerate. If you believe a treatment will work, please have the decency to ask if you can suggest it. My advice? If you want to suggest something, simply ask, are you open to suggestions? If the answer is no, thank you, then ask what can I do to help? Or what do you need me to do?

For Brian and me, all the friendly – oftentimes unhelpful – advice was just salt into a wound that was never going to heal. For his part, he was a 100% conventional medicine man. No complementary therapies. No out there treatments. No witch's brew, thank you. He even eschewed the hospital's psychologist.

It was left to me to explain to friends that he trusted the oncologists, the radiologists, the nurse practitioners and then, ultimately, the palliative care nurses, to best take care of his needs. Once the prognosis was given, we knew it was only Brian's strength of character that would make the coming few months of radiation and chemo doable.

Brian needed to be cared for the way he wanted. Reasonable? Absolutely.

Note to Self: The star performer may, or may not, want to be centre stage.

After the initial blasts of radiation and six weeks of chemo, we waited. He began having chest pains. A lung operation confirmed the worst – it had metastasised. We discussed telling our broader friendship groups the prognosis was bad. Except that Brian, looking as though death's door was a long way off, didn't want to. I told him I'd be calling his mates and asking them to come up to The Valley to see him, to say hi – and goodbye. He was having none of it. There was no way he was going to be paraded out, feeling like shit, for all and sundry to come and give him sad, pitying looks. No way. Our previously upbeat conversations about a living funeral had long since sunk.

I told him how much he was loved. Then, I was brutal. I said: 'You're a long time dead. Do you think these people will thank me for keeping your imminent death from them?' It took a while to sink in. The inevitable was accepted.

Brian had quite a few friendship groups: the school mates, the work blokes, the golf guys, the hang gliders, the adopted family, the first wife's group, the second wife's group. Often these overlapped: I was the second wife's group and a part of the school mates. The school buds were often the golf group. You get the gist. For reasons he kept to himself, there were only two people I wasn't allowed to contact: an ex-partner and his hang-glider pilot instructor. There were also only two people I was unable to contact; and it wasn't for a lack of trying and some amazing investigative work on my part; alas John the millionaire and Greg the mechanic remained uninformed. Our siblings were there from the get-go. Thankfully, both our mothers had died within ten days of each other the year prior. Our dads had long gone.

I do acknowledge the parade was awful for him. Throughout, he was brave and full of bravado. He was patient and in pain. He sang and offered solace. At the end of each visit, he was exhausted, but ultimately sated by the realisation the tiredness was cancer combined with love, friendship, respect, and admiration. I firmly believe in the importance of being able to freely express how you feel about a loved one dying; to tell them and show gratitude and love. It is very hard to say, 'Hey, I want you to know how much I'm going to miss you. I just want to say thank you and share this memory with you.' You can't beat around the bush – especially if you know there's not much time. Just say it. Brian knew his time was depleting. His body was telling him in no uncertain terms.

On the day we had the old boys' co-worker visits, one came up to me and said, 'You know, I'm older than him. When I first started working with Brian, he put so much faith in me. He taught me. I remember thinking – he's a youngster but I'm learning from him. He's a great bloke. I'll miss him.' Another interjected, saying 'Bullshit! I never wanted to be like him: he was an arsehole – but only at work. I admired him in every other facet of his life. Just not at work: he was a shithead.' My god, we laughed.

I was able to reach Brian's first wife, Lil, and ask her to come up. I was so glad I did. Watching them from the kitchen window, leaning in to share a memory, he gently touched her knee. Their easy intimacy erasing the heartache of the past. She had broken his heart. I marvelled at the man. He carried no ill will toward anyone. Of everyone in our social circle of forty years ago, Brian and Lil were the couple I admired most. Strangely, it didn't feel odd that, decades later, we'd be supporting our husband. We both benefitted from his love, care, and strength. Lil and I held each other and had a small cry.

And the parade? Exhausting as it was, it turned out he didn't mind because he knew, in the end, he was destined for a long sleep.

Note to Self: You think you're not feeling but you are.

Brian believed getting up each day was imperative. And he did. Every day. He refused to see it from a prone position. Every day, but for his last four, he got up.

The two of us had agreed how this would happen. Because he was so thin with almost no muscular strength, his daily rising was an ordeal. The method, finely tuned over a few weeks of trying, had been successful in ensuring minimal pain. A support handle was attached to the bed base. And on the side table, the morphine, and the syringe. I would hold his lower and upper arm in a kind of monkey grip, and pull his poor skeletal frame upright, while he transferred his legs by swinging them around the support handle which he held in his left hand.

One morning we had words. It was in the last few days of his life at home. We'd been doing the same getting out of bed manoeuvre for endless days. But this morning, no, we got only so far when he fell back onto the pillow, breathless, grey, and moist. He screamed blue murder at me: your fault, your fault, your fault!! I stood there, mute. It felt like a freight train had barrelled past me, taking all the air in the room and me with it. I thought I felt nothing. I whispered, 'That wasn't what we agreed,' and walked out.

We tried again later, maybe fifteen minutes later. And nailed it. It was never brought up again.

The feeling of nothing; no thing. I wonder what that is. Because although I felt nothing, I was aware that I felt no thing. What is that? I don't know. Is it the letting go?

Note to Self: Not everyone's a wordsmith.

Sometimes, when I think back on the time before Brian died, I feel denied. I felt there were times wasted and opportunities lost. I asked for his participation to help his children cope with losing him. I asked him to think about their future and how it would look without him in it and how he could help alleviate their distress. I needed him to help me create a space that supported their grief by being there in spirit.

I often felt like a stage manager in those nine months: arranging things that could be looked back upon with joy or yearning. I wanted our children to feel no moments of regret – only that there weren't enough moments.

Our son needed day surgery. I had arranged it to take place a week prior to the May school holiday break. He would be at home an extra week, yippee. I spoke with Xavier, saying it would be a great time to explain to his dad Day Z, Minecraft, and all the other computer games he loved. I suggested to Brian he could teach his fifteen-year-old Chess, Backgammon and the few card tricks he knew. Maybe show him how to play the didgeridoo if it didn't hurt his lungs too much. Or get him started on the guitar, uke or harmonica. It didn't happen; Brian had no interest in computer games and Elliott had no interest in learning to play an instrument. They did, however, spend a lot of time with Neil Young. Their shared admiration for *Prairie Wind* held me spellbound, their harmonies, mellifluous.

Eighteen-year-old Tilly was away at uni in Wagga Wagga. I asked Brian to write to her. To talk to her through letters or emails. I asked him to say how wonderful it was that she was studying so hard and how proud he was of her achievements. Compliment her talents, especially her musical and artistic abilities. To share a newfound song or a joke. He didn't because they were peas in a pod; they lived for the joy they gave each other. He did not want to hurt her, all the while knowing his cancer was inflicting unintentional pain. No amount of teasing and silly behaviour, no words, would heal the aching hurt she was experiencing.

Lil and Brian separated because of his intense desire for a family. His own upbringing was fraught, to say the least. Our children were more important to him than life. I say that very deliberately. He'd have given his heart to them, absolutely.

It was for this reason, I asked him to write a letter to each of them; to tell them the things he'd wish for them, how much they meant to him, talk about his dreams for them. I wanted him to tell them what he was scared and not scared about, of how much he'd miss not seeing them grow, fall in love, marry (or not), have kids of their own (or not), how much he wanted to be a Poppy. He couldn't because his heart was broken.

I asked him to write a letter to me so I'd have something I could read when the shit hit the fan. When I was lost and missing him, and remembering the man he was. Of the dreams he'd held and lost, held, and won. And simply how much I meant to him. He didn't because his broken heart didn't need to be shattered, too.

Ahead we had Tilly's 21st, Xavier's high school graduation, first Christmas, his birthday, first Fathers' Day without him: I had nothing from their dad to give them on those special days.

He wasn't a poet or a wordsmith. I didn't expect him to be. He could have easily jagged a few lines from Clayton, Young or McCartney. We three would know they weren't originals. We'd understand why. We'd have something. It made me angry then. It made me feel I had failed them.

Note to Self: All minutiae of your life are not memorable, but a memory can be found in minutiae.

One morning, pre-dawn, we sat quietly in our lounge room looking through the triple glassed doors across to the Watagan Ranges waiting for the sun to rise. We didn't say anything. Just sat. Holding hands. Breathing breaths; his tortured and mine fearful. I didn't know what he was thinking. I imagined he'd be waiting for all this to pass. He wasn't afraid of dying. He hated the pain. He was embarrassed by his cancer-ridden body. He was angry it had let him down. We usually weren't up this early. Most mornings we'd wake after sunrise; and he would swear. What the fuck? I'm awake. I'm still here. Most mornings I'd lie there and wait for his gasping breath and know he was about to say, 'What the fuck. I'm awake. I'm still here!'

He sat closest to the glass, gazing out. His eyes never lost their cerulean blue. They were sunken, though. His face was ashen and wizened. His nose now too big for his face. He was sixty-one. We locked hands the way we always did and just breathed. I'm not sure how long we sat there. We sat, like an old, old couple in our dressing gowns, holding hands, saying things to each other without opening our mouths. No verbalising. I think just realising.

We held hands, always. Like my parents, we were the hand holding couple. Unlike a lot of our friends. In the supermarket. Out on walks. At the movies. Everywhere. I liked holding his hand. There was a surety in it. A sense of belonging. I remember how his hands felt the first time he took mine in his; our hands fitted so naturally together; we had turned to each other and smiled a smile of recognition. Strangely, his hands were like my mother's. Somewhat gnarly; thick, but not fat, fingers; and tidy square nails; strong but not calloused. He used them a lot; to hold faces, to make love, to play music, to wash and cuddle babies, to garden and to mend things. Now his hands were a rag taggle bunch of bones held together by a transparent voile of grey, white and knitted lines of blue.

In that pre-dawn, holding hands, I felt I was offering him a surety, of what I didn't know. Perhaps he knew he'd be gone in days.

It was the last morning of August. Outside, the liquid amber – bare, stark, and lonely – broke the sunlight of an aging winter as it made its way into the room. I wondered if I was ever going to be warm again.

Adventure Faces

Hannah May

Even if I had never seen this photo before, I would know that it is my mum. It's the way that she props her knee up, with her feet clad in the snug brown leather boots. The way she wears those big purple wool socks that bunch above the rim. I imagine her face as she stares out at the fjord. She has little creases in her eyebrows and her lips are pressed tightly together as if she is trying to solve something complex. Inside her head is a scattered pattern of maps, topography, memories from other landscapes. She estimates the distance to the peak in front of her, and wonders if she can convince my dad to do 'just a quick side trip'. She asks him gleefully while they make peanut butter wraps. Dad laughs. He knows her optimism well.

This photo marks the last adventure my parents had before children. In 1995, they were ready to start a family, but it meant saying a temporary goodbye to the hiking trips they loved. They booked a trip to New Zealand and walked the Routeburn Track together. Ten months later, my brother was born. My sister and I followed in the years after that, and my parents' overseas hikes were downscaled to kid-friendly bushwalks.

When I was fourteen, Mum introduced me to hiking. We drove to the Victorian high country, up through dirt mountain roads with no safety barriers against the edge. Mum wore the same hiking pack from the photo in 1995. As we walked over an alpine ridge, she told me that her and Dad bought those packs with the last $500 leftover after their wedding. They got married, spent the last of their money on hiking packs, and then house-sat after their honeymoon until they could afford rent.

'Really?' I said. I watched mum's thick socks and brown leather boots as I walked behind her. 'But Dad's always so worried about money.' I thought back to when he took me shopping for my new school uniform at the start of year seven. I wanted three of the white sports shirts. That's what Charlie was getting. But when I looked at Dad checking the price tags with wide eyes, I sadly put two back on the rack.

I see a lot of Mum in myself. A few months ago, Abe and I were standing on the rock shelf behind the Newcastle baths. We were at that in-between stage of a relationship – that time when you know how much fun you're having together, but you're too scared to bring it up. The waves were over five foot and crashing onto the rock ledge. I saw a handrail that was built around a crevice in the rocks. With each big wave, the water surged along the channel, up between the rocks until it lapped around the metal.

'Do you want to go and hold on to the rail?' I looked up at Abe. He was in his board shorts, with his face all crinkled as he laughed at me.

'It sounds as though you really want to. And that makes it impossible for me to say no!' He followed me out towards the railing, and we clung on as the waves tried to pull us into the ocean.

At the beginning of this year, my parents went backpacking in South America. They planned to be away for at least six months. My sister had finished school, and they were ready to try out another trip together. We had no idea that COVID-19 would change the world in a few short weeks. I went home for the weekend to say goodbye and drive them to the airport. On the morning that they left, Mum bounced around the house. She showed me all her new hiking gear, including the new packs that she bought for herself and Dad. The old ones had fallen apart.

'Look!' She grinned at Dad as he came through the doorway into the kitchen. 'Dad even bought himself a new hiking shirt.'

I smiled at Dad. He looked more relaxed than that day in the uniform shop. He was softer. Dad showed me all the pockets on his new shirt. He had stuffed them all full of snacks and hankies. He looked like a dag, but I loved him for it.

There was a childishness about my parents that morning that I hadn't seen for years.

'Hey, Jo?' Dad turned to Mum during breakfast.

'Yeah?'

'Want to go to South America with me?'

'Oh, okay! When?' Mum sounded rehearsed.

'How about today?'

'Let's do it!' They laughed together, and I laughed at them.

Four of us drove to the airport: Mum, Dad, my little sister, and me. Dad checked his pockets repeatedly for their passports. Mum looked out the windows and told us all about Santiago.

We helped them check in their bags. As we got to the boarding gate, everyone stopped talking. I looked at Mum and Dad. Dad touched all his pockets and adjusted his carry-on bag straps. Mum just burst into tears. Dad stopped what he was doing, and he was in tears as well.

When my sister and I drove back to my parents' house, I went straight to their room. I slid open Mum's wardrobe. In the hanger, there were pairs of thick wool socks rolled together. Purple, red, yellow and green. The wool was pulled and fluffy. I squeezed them all, then stuffed the red pair into my pocket.

I can still imagine Mum's face back in 1995, as she convinced Dad to climb an extra mountain. But now I can picture his face too. It is the same face he made at breakfast. The corners of his mouth tilting upwards, as he tries to suppress a smile. His intense playful eyes. A little shoulder lift. 'Want to go to South America with me?'

An Unflattering Family Portrait

Jackson Driver

I couldn't believe how large she looked. I'd been flipping through the pages of a family photo album, looking for something to write about, when the picture of my youthful parents – my mum looking oh-so chunky – leaped out and struck me. Indeed, I was so rocked by this image that I promptly closed the entire album, placed it in a shelf under my desk, and didn't dare peer at it again for an entire two weeks.

Upon returning to the photo, I deduced that it had been taken on Christmas day of 1992: almost exactly five months after my mum had given birth to my big brother Ben, and (I suppose, though I'd rather not dwell on it) right around the time she fell pregnant with me. She was twenty-three then – four years younger than I am now – and probably weighed around a hundred kilos. Shocking.

Don't misunderstand me: I'm certainly not being critical. You see, historically, I was always a big fellow. As far back as infant school, I was very much the fat kid of the class (as well as the nerd, the clown, the *Star Wars* freak, and many other more-successfully-repressed monikers). On weekends, I would go with my family to the local footy field, where both of my brothers would strap on their headgear and enthusiastically lead their respective teams into battle; while I, with a similar enthusiasm, would hurry to the tuck shop and struggle to decide between a Mars Bar and a packet of cheese and onion chips. From the sidelines, my parents would watch every minute of every game with genuine interest, all the while mingling with the other kids' parents who would go on to become their closest friends. Meanwhile, I'd find myself a tree to sit under, crack into a *Jedi Apprentice* novel, and await the magical final scream of the horn that signalled it was time to go home.

Yes, I was always the bulky black sheep in a family of active sports fans – and I always saw my mum as very much being 'one of them'. Now that I think back on it, I do recall her struggling with her weight when I was very little: attending Weight Watchers meetings; counting calories in a little notepad; cooking herself separate, lighter dinners … But, to me, this was only ever a minor quirk, and had more to do with her being a woman than with her being particularly unhealthy. I never thought of her as being truly fat: I never thought of her as being like me.

More recently, I've managed to shed much of my weight, becoming quite slim indeed. All in all, I've lost something like forty kilograms (though an exact figure is hard to confirm, as there were a good few years in my early twenties when I refused to ever weigh myself). Partially, I was able to achieve this massive feat by cutting down my bread intake and opting to walk instead of drive whenever possible. Mostly though, the credit belongs to marijuana, with which, upon moving out of home five years ago, I very quickly replaced my daily indulgence of sweet-treats.

Which, in an admittedly long-winded sort of way, brings me back to my mum … She has quite a colourful family background, I've always thought. When she was a teenager, her mother (orphaned when she was ten, by way of a freak gas leak), divorced her father. As I understand it, this was largely due to his being an abusive alcoholic, which, in turn, was a result of his pent-up rage at having had polio as a boy, and now being reliant on crutches to walk. Later, he was sent to jail for creating multiple fake welfare accounts, causing him to miss my parents' wedding. Upon his release, he reformed, began working as a chat-line councillor, and, at some point, married a mail-order bride from the Philippines: the mother of my 'aunt' Carmel, older than me by four years. So, as I said, quite a colourful family background.

I didn't notice that either of my parents were above-averagely fond of wine until I was about sixteen; and it wasn't for a while later that I found out that cask wine is considered low-class. Both drank about equally, but my dad definitely handled it better. At worst, he would fall asleep before the movie finished, or forget to close the kitchen door after refilling his glass while I was trying to sleep. Mum though … she would become unpleasantly loud – screechy, even – and talk your head off about utter nonsense; inevitably becoming offended when she recognised others' embarrassment, and quick to defend herself by slinging major insults with minor warning. Quite frankly, I found it disgusting, and for a long while, it put me off drinking altogether: I lasted a whole six months of being eighteen without having a single drop. Of course, then I grew up …

And now, here I sit, photo album in my lap, looking at my massive mum from nine months before I was born. It never occurred to me that we might be so similar. I can't help but wonder if the wine wasn't integral to her weight-loss, as the weed was for mine. I wonder if it made other things easier as well: like her contentment with being a stay-at-home mother of three boys; or her continued, supportive relationship with her increasingly disabled father. I wonder too if one day I'll have children of my own, only for them to grow embarrassed and disgusted by whatever substance I'm hooked on twenty years from now. Time will tell, I suppose. If things do pan out that way, and my future children ever come across a photo of me looking my largest, I wonder if they'll wonder. I hope to hell they do.

ABC News and other Bedtime Lullabies

Hannah McGregor

It is not uncommon (although far from a daily occurrence) that you will find me bragging about being a light sleeper. As if waking up to a dog bark or a creaky floorboard is akin to that raving review you got for your very first amateur play. Perhaps it is the thought of being able to wake up during an emergency that gives me a sense of superiority, some intrinsic or remanent survival instinct. Or it could be because of the pleasantness and rarity of being called light as opposed to heavy. Heavy body, heavy mind, heavy heart – it gets rather tiresome, it can really weigh you down.

What I am less willing to admit to is that, in order to fall asleep, I require vast amounts of planning, fluffing, and the cosiest set of pyjamas. I fail to mention the three blankets, four pillows and five mattress toppers that protect me from the terrifying world. Perhaps the most interesting aspect of my sleeping habit is the newest. I can only fall asleep if I leave the ABC news on in the background.

Now I know what you're thinking: that's not curious or unusual, many people require ambient noise to sleep. People leave fans on, or keep the window open just to hear the traffic go past. There are even white noise machines you can buy! Knowing your objections, I must specify that it is only the ABC News that will let me peacefully drift off. I have tirelessly experimented.

Perhaps it is the sound of a voice that calms me? Surely music would be an appropriate substitution?

No.

Or another less strange and depressing television program? What about Gardening Australia?

No.

Fine, what about WIN news? OR SBS news? What is the difference? I honestly do not know.

At this stage we must question: what is the harm of listening to the news to go to sleep? If I am able to sleep, surely that is a positive. And if it brings me comfort, can it really be a problem?

And, for those who question how death, war, disease, and disaster can be comforting, I suggest that (in a world where these exact things are so prevalent) perhaps the only way to take comfort in it, is to be aware and expect the worst.

Maybe one day I'll be able to sleep without the ABC news; the silence of the unknown will not be terrifying; and the three blankets, four pillows and five mattress toppers will be enough.

Or maybe they won't.

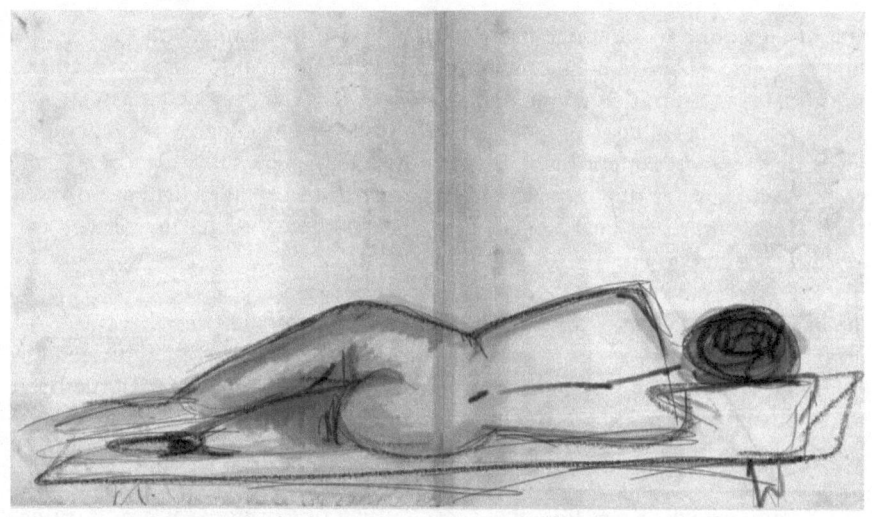

Curiosities Uncovered

Hannah McGregor

Everyone has curiosities. Mine is that I can't pronounce the 'th' sound. It only affects specific words like third, thirst and three. My tongue is the problem, it refuses to cooperate.

Rather than naturally gliding across my top teeth, it decides to stick to the familiar landscape of my mouth. I can fight it, but it's hard and uncomfortable, and I have to be really concentrating.

I have never been embarrassed by it; it was never an insecurity of mine. In school, it was just a point of conversation, something occasionally raised by teachers. At home my mother, an English teacher, was worried I had missed a developmental stage or been influenced by other accents when we moved countries. She sent me to a literacy specialist. After the lessons stopped, so did any mention of my fronting of 'th'.

A week or two ago, a friend who studies teaching was telling me about speech impediments, and absentmindedly said, 'You know it's just like yours.' This shouldn't be surprising, of course she would notice, she was being taught to observe and correct this exact type of thing.

I decided the story was fantastic; here I was, twenty-one and having completely forgotten my own inability to pronounce a simple sound. So, I decided to tell another friend, Sophia.

Leaning against a rusty pole, in the dwindling light, waiting for our fish and chips, I repeated the encounter with unrelenting hand gestures and a little bit of exaggeration. 'And then she points out I have one! It's so subtle though, but I guess since she's learning about them ...'

I went on to offer the same explanation that I gave you, the spiel about which words I can say and which ones I can't, as well as numerous demonstrations.

Sophia looked at me and uncomfortably blurted out, 'Hannah, I know; I noticed when we first met. I didn't mention it in case you were embarrassed.'

I was stunned.

That was two separate people in my life who were aware of my encumbrance without my involvement. I was mortified. Not that I couldn't pronounce 'th', but because I thought it was something unnoticeable, something which was concealed under fast talking, something that I had become unaware of.

These conversations make me question what else has been noticed. Have things I desperately tried to hide been observed? Or do I have more curiosities that I am oblivious to?

I guess I'll find out.

Vehementi

Hannah McGregor

Admittingly, I project myself as being a non-confrontational, anti-violence, lefty. Someone who doesn't like the military, Australian drinking culture (and associated aggression), or the excuse 'boys will be boys', and yet, my default response in tough situations is to fight.

My mother filled my childhood, and my sister's, with stories of defending her friends and sticking up for herself. My favourite is from when my mum was in year five. She reached into her pencil case, sharpened her pencil, and launched it into the unexpecting arm of the schoolyard bully – a girl who had been intimidating my mum and her friends on their walk home for a whole year.

My father is the opposite. You could describe him as a pacifist. The other day he was sitting in the car talking to me on the phone, describing what he had been up to. A woman, meanwhile, was trying to squeeze her trolley between his car and another one. My dad was getting increasingly worried she wouldn't fit. Excusing himself, he got out of the car. I could hear him faintly ask her to try to find a different path. When he returned, he was on edge. Recounting it to my mother she was shocked, 'That's unusual for him.'

Even though I idolise Martin Luther King Jr. and Tom Hayden's approach to conflict, I have adopted my mother's more violent approach to confrontation. I punched my first and only (I felt I should clarify that) person when I was fifteen. After a week of endless taunts and other annoying behaviour, I was over it. 'Don't do it again, or I will hit you.'

Blood trickled down over his top lip into his mouth.

His hand clutched his nose, and his eyes began to well up.

He was embarrassed, probably because I was a girl, so he didn't tell on me. The group that had encircled us were all on my side, sparing me from any serious repercussions. I never told my parents, and I don't mention it when I talk about my non-violent preference. I prefer for my outburst to remain private, allowing me to avoid hypocrisy. But, in order for you to understand fully what I struggle with, you needed to know.

When I think about how I would react given a similar situation, I am always torn between ideals and actions, justice and appropriateness. I'm scared of what I will do, what I want to do, and what I should do.

Two Attempts

Alice Connors

Here is how the second attempt went:

Mum was sitting out the back having a smoke. We'd agreed to watch *Thor: Ragnarok,* a movie Angus insisted she would love. I didn't disagree, she's just a hard person to pin down. But first, the cigarette.

Angus brought me out a watermelon cider. It tasted like lollies and made me really feel like I was home. Not because I'd drunk one before – this was a novelty – but because the lolly shop in town sold little watermelon lollies for ten cents each. When I was young, I'd never have more than two dollars on hand. I suppose not a lot has changed.

We had been talking about something unimportant before, but interesting. I think Mum was trying to convince us to watch *That Sugar Film,* because it blew her mind and changed her worldview. This was not the first time she'd beaten that drum, and something in the way she spoke, lifted the stubborn edge she gave Angus and me.

Maybe it was the drink, maybe the view of the forest trees, or the smell of home, but I didn't feel like fighting. I placated her by saying I'd watch it in my spare time.

She said something after that, something along the lines of, 'You're a good boy.' Not that, but similar.

And I decided to take the shot.

I'd thought of it earlier that day, walking into town. I asked my partner, and she thought it was a good idea. She's cleverer than me. So, I had it pretty firm in my mind, but never thought I'd do it.

But here I was.

'Actually, there's something I've been meaning to talk about.'

Silence.

'It's kind of serious, is everyone okay with me being serious?'

They gave some noises of assent.

'I'm not a boy.'

Mum nodded and looked away.

'I mentioned it once when I was younger, and you didn't take it very well. I've thought about it a lot and just wanted to let you know again: I'm not a boy.'

She caught my gaze for a moment and nodded again.

Angus spoke up. 'Yeah, I remember you saying something years ago and I've wondered how that's been progressing.'

I looked at him. 'I did, and it's been more or less the same. I'm a girl or non-binary or something. It's complicated.'

Mum said, 'Complicated how? What does that mean?'

I think this is when I stopped being afraid. She wasn't angry, she wasn't confused, she was curious. She was just curious.

I explained some ideas – the gender binary, pronouns, sexual preference and identity. It was all rote to me. Maybe I didn't explain enough, but she's not great at listening.

'So, does this mean you'll date boys now?'

It was such an innocent question.

'Yeah, if I want to. I don't really judge based on gender whether I like someone.'

We got into an argument after this. Don't take this to mean a bad thing, that's how we communicate. I told her that I tended not to like boys because we didn't have anything in common: they like sports and cars and I very much don't. She told me I couldn't judge someone based on those surface details. The irony of this was lost on her.

The argument went away. Angus was doing his best to act impartially, changing the subject and injecting humour.

'I support you,' Mum said. 'Whatever you need to do, I'm here for you.'

The crying didn't start here.

'Thank you. That means a lot. You made it very hard for me when I was a kid, having to hide this.'

It didn't start for a little while.

'I had so much to deal with! Your father had died, and you were so depressed, you weren't handling it well, and then you piled this on top and it was just too much for me to handle!'

The irony of that statement was lost on her too.

'You made it worse, Mum. If you'd just accepted me, the depression wouldn't have been so bad.'

She sniffled. 'I didn't know that.'

It took me a little while to work up to it.

'I want an apology.'

This started a new argument. Angus's impartiality left for a little while. Mum said that she was from another time, that 'most people' don't interact with someone like me their whole life. Angus reiterated that, said that she was good compared to other people her age. This went on longer than the last argument.

I said, 'Please, just let me talk.'

They nodded.

'A person's origin, their upbringing, the things you're talking about, they can explain why they did something. They do not excuse them.'

Did I cry first or Mum?

'If you had accepted me, it would have made things easier. I could have transitioned. I could have fixed this earlier, and I wouldn't hate myself every time I look in the mirror.'

Regardless, we were both crying now.

She did that old person thing where you say 'I apologise' without actually apologising. The words 'from the bottom of my heart' were in there too.

'I support anything you need to do.'

That was the second attempt. After that we got into another argument about something, Mum poured us some rum and we watched *Thor*. She did like it. She kept saying 'I need a man like that,' about Chris Hemsworth.

The first attempt is harder to pin down.

Its edges are sharp and hook into nearby trauma. It blends with another memory, a small one but similar: let's call it a false start. I'll tell that first as I remember it more clearly. Maybe that'll help sift out the parts that don't belong.

My room was right next to the toilet. This was convenient, most of the time. When it wasn't, I would just turn up my music to drown out the sounds of plopping.

I must have been on the toilet, going through Facebook on my phone. I can only imagine what sort of brick-phone I had at thirteen.

On that toilet, mind half focused on the scrolling screen, my little heart was torn in half. I must have gone into hysterics, screaming, and crying. I remember the conversation happening through the bathroom door, Mum leant up against the other side, yelling, struggling with her bad hearing.

'What's wrong? Is everything okay?'

I made a garbled sound, an attempt at language.

'What? You're gay? Oh pumpkin, it's okay that you're gay! You know I support you …'

I opened the door between us. 'No, it's Renee! She has a new boyfriend.'

Renee, my first love, the girl that I'd dated for two weeks.

To her credit, Mum did not laugh.

This was the first great trauma my mind could comprehend. I think if Mum had known that, then she would have handled it better. She held me and told me it would be okay, but I could feel her simmer.

Something about broken expectations always set her off. She let me be sad for a day before she was fed up. She snapped, and told me it didn't mean anything. Small jabs aimed at boosting my confidence.

I must not have been happy until I was in my next relationship. I came home beaming. When I told Mum why, she said, 'I don't like how you have to be with someone to be happy.'

Dad had given me the romantic genes. That's what I thought at the time.

Even as I told that story, another was folded out, connected to it like a twin. The first attempt must have happened after this, because I remember telling my second girlfriend about my dad's death.

So, it's after the second girlfriend, after the death, the depression. Maybe I'd started seeing my therapist, maybe I was fixated on someone else. I had friends, at least I thought I did.

We were a little quartet. Odd kids, funny kids. We tried our hardest not to care how people thought of us. Cody did that with niche hobbies and fancy clothes. Sid by morose tone and off-kilter jokes. Raph posted hentai to his Facebook profile.

You take what you can get, for a little while.

They were all queer, in the very modern sense. Sid was very open about being bisexual, and for someone who had barely kissed another person, that was a shock to me. All three of them were hypersexual.

One of the things that confused my mum the most was how out of the blue it was. One day I was a 'normal kid' and then this. A lot of my younger childhood is lost to me, but my theory is that I had just never considered it. When I made these loud, confident, different friends, I started to consider it for the first time.

They all turned out to be terrible people. Raph creeped on every girl he met, Cody hooked up with my at-the-time girlfriend (who he later married), and Sid. Well, Sid's some sort of Men's Rights Activist.

This is the world I'm in when I come home that day. It happened a nice way. Mum came into my room to chat, sat on my bed. After a while I said I had to tell her something.

'I think I'm a girl.'

'No, you're not.'

'I've never felt like a boy. I've been thinking and ...'

Raised voices still make me shrink.

'You were such a normal kid!'

Those sharp edges pull the surface of the memory.

'I just want you to have a normal life!'

The screaming is infectious.

'You can't do this to me!'

We didn't talk about it. I would wear a scarf as a skirt in the mirror, sweating in fear that Mum would come home. The screaming didn't stop. I started thinking that any conversation had a timer ticking away, counting down the seconds until we were shouting.

I had respite from Mum's ire once. My stepmum, Sue, is a sporadic sort of supportive. I'd mentioned it to her in passing and she carried that information with her. One day I was visiting, and she asked me what I was doing on the weekend. I said I had nothing planned so she told me her idea.

I was very nervous. It felt like coming home, in a way. Like meeting long lost family.

The house was very grand. Wealthy, with a beach view. I felt like my presence alone would break something.

There was a long period of awkwardness before the woman arrived. Some fear and shame welled up because she didn't pass, she looked masculine in spite of her effort. I felt so sorry for having that thought.

She was the first transgender person I had seen in the flesh. I don't remember her name. She, her partner Sue, and I had lunch together. They did all the talking.

After a long time, there was a lull, and she turned to me.

'Do you have any questions?'

I don't remember if I did.

I thanked her and her partner when we left. I thanked Sue in the car. It was a quiet ride home.

Mum found out. She didn't like that we went behind her back. She and Sue are friends but your ex-husband's partner making secret plans with your child must not feel good. More screaming.

Those are all the pieces stuck to the sides of the first attempt, near-enough. That lump rests at the back of my head, always burning.

Today I woke up in my partner's bed. She woke up before me, which is rare. While I was still in the throes of sleep, she put her arms around me.

She said, 'I'm so glad I get to wake up next to my girlfriend.'

She calls me her girlfriend as often as she can.

I feel guilty every time, but I'm getting better at it. It's like learning to accept compliments all over again.

She buys me dresses and tells me what I look good in. She shows me how the things she takes for granted work. She says I'm beautiful and pretty and soft. I've never felt more confident.

In a few weeks I'm going to talk to my therapist about testosterone blockers. I think I'll go onto estrogen eventually, laser off all the hair, get into shape.

Here's a third attempt:

We go out to a cafe. It's late in the afternoon but we have a reservation.

The man smiles as we turn up.

I say, 'Table for two, for Alice?'

He looks down, 'Yes, got you right here. Follow me.'

We sit and he brings over some menus.

'How are we today, ladies?'

'Good thank you, how are you?'

'I'm very well! Can I start you with drinks?'

I raise a finger. 'First, do you have a bathroom?'

'Just at the end of the hall.'

I take my time. There's a girl in there washing her hands. I smile at her and she smiles back.

My love and I order drinks and a meal to share.

While she's off in the bathroom, I pay the bill.

We leave holding hands.

Responding with a Click

Lucy Neilson–Spitzer

The sky bleeds orange and pink as the sun rises. The air is chilly, it nips at me as I wheel the bins out into the forecourt. I really don't want to be here today. It's six a.m.; once that seemed too early to work, but now I've adapted to the morning fog. Although, the resilience doesn't make me any more excited to spend the next seven hours here. I know Chloe will come at eleven, but I'll have to run the shop by myself until then.

And there are already customers lining up outside of the BP, looking towards me expectantly. They stare me down as I arduously lug the bins to their bay. If they want to enter the shop faster, they could just offer to help.

Once these outside jobs are done, the day begins to shuffle along. People collect their newspapers, lotto is bought, and rolls are made. I don't really think, just kind of react. My body moves out of instinct, seeing a customer and serving them absentmindedly. Like a shadow following the body, my mind hangs at the cracked soles of my shoes. My thoughts become the lowest priority.

I find it somehow strange that I no longer pay attention when serving the customers. A man comes in for lotto. He is old and bearded and completely average. In his hand is a blue piece of paper. He reads from the long list of orders.

'A maxi pick for Powerball,' I click a button.

'Twenty-four games for Oz lotto,' again I click.

'And ... thirty-six for Saturday.' Click.

But I'm not paying attention, my mind has dulled. I hear what he says shallowly, responding accordingly. The job gets done. He pays, handing me three fifty-dollar notes and I do the maths blankly. He leaves the shop and it's on to the next person.

I summarise her order in a click.

I watch the clock. It's 10:45 – Chloe will be here any minute. I like to consider myself a punctual person, I'm subservient to time. If I tell myself the bacon and egg rolls must be cooked by 5:30 then they'll be cooked by 5:30. I set parameters within which I must abide.

Chloe is different though. She dances around time.

It becomes 10:50 … still no Chloe. The lotto machine has the exact time, seconds and all (currently 10:50:36). It hurts to watch. I suppose it's like watching paint dry or grass grow – a boring cliché to centre myself around.

Soon she walks in the door.

'Hi Chloe!' I say.

'Hey Lucy,' she responds.

She clocks on, the little boxy machine taking a few times to register her fingerprint. Eventually it turns green and gives her a small beep of acceptance.

'How are you?' I ask.

'Good.' She goes to put on her apron and the top of it gets caught on her blotchy, pale pink hair.

'You all good if I dash off to the bathroom real quick?' I ask, colloquial and seemingly relaxed. As if I'm not dying for a break.

She nods and I truly do dash towards the backrooms of the BP.

They are dark, illuminated by flat flashing lights. No one (myself included) ever bothers to turn the lights on, so the space is constantly filled with nothing but that dull orange colour that's saved for emergencies and evacuations. Even the machines seem tired, their beeps hollow and languid. Or maybe the beeps of the main shop area are too loud and enthusiastic.

I twist around milk crates, oil vats and dusty cartons of cleaning products. I make it into the toilet. It's small and vaguely smells of dead ants. I'm not claustrophobic but here it feels as if the walls are slowly pressing together. Like, if I closed my eyes for too long, I'd find myself sandwiched between them.

Up goes my apron, down my pants and sit on the toilet. The flimsy plastic rim is cool against skin, my thighs expanding upon touchdown. I put my head in my hands and sit a second. That's all. I just sit and see how long I can delay heading back to the constant questions and demands.

I recharge.

Work has ended and I hobble away from its walls. The sky is now a dusty blue. The vibrant colours of the morning have muted. My car is easily spotted. It's a dulled yellow and requires no energy to find. I try to shake myself into alertness, but I'm spent. Exhausting the body exhausts the mind.

As I drive, my mind wanders. It goes nowhere in particular. Yet it isn't present. My body still reacts on instinct. I indicate and turn down the usual streets. The car responds in hurried ticks and clicks.

I drive past the Waratah High School (Callaghan Technology Campus, is it?) and suddenly I'm struck with an awfully spontaneous idea: why don't I stop and get some snacks? Just from Coles.

It takes a second for me to think it through. Is there enough time? Enough money? Am I too tired? Is it too late to change into the other lane?

It's decided that I deserve a treat so quickly the car pulls into the right lane, my attention suddenly back on the road. I indicate and turn into the Waratah Coles parking lot. The park is close to Coles, where the spaces are small and sparse. I could've parked further away, there are lots of parks a short walk from the shops. But then I'd have to walk.

I struggle to pull into one of the ashy, cubic spaces. It's tight, wonky. A bit of reversing and it straightens up. I couldn't get it perfect but decide to leave it. There's only a small slant. Besides, I'll be back in under ten minutes.

Hurriedly, I enter Coles. It's very red. The aisle signs are red, the uniforms are red – even the trollies have red. It's angry and hurts my eyes. Why do supermarkets need such abrasively monocoloured marketing?

Maybe this is why I prefer to shop at Aldi.

I head straight to aisle number six – the chip aisle. I slow down. I peruse. Dragging my feet down the length, my eyes scan the products. But assessing the options quickly grows boring. I go to the Smiths section, which by far garners the best chips. I look over the flavours. Usually I'd be inclined to have Cheese and Onion. It is my favourite after all. But maybe switching things up and going for Salt and Vinegar would be good. Or even the classic Original. It's a hard choice.

My hand reaches for the familiar yellow packaging and, before I even know it, my choice is made. You can't go wrong with your favourite. Cheese and Onion, it is. The bag is bloated and crinkles loudly under my grip. I walk to the self-serve registers and it scans easily. I carry it back to my car.

Eventually I'm home. I head up towards my apartment. I like to note the varying smells each time while climbing up the stairs. Now the air smells dank, probably mirroring the last person to walk up. How will it smell to the next person, the person who'll climb after me?

I've reached my door. It's a dirty cream colour, garnished with a rusted number fourteen. I fiddle around for the key. Opening the door is a two-hand operation. One hand on the handle, the other on the key as it twists into the lock. Simultaneously, I pull the door handle forward and twist some more. There is an almost silent click. Then it unlocks.

When I first moved into the apartment, it would take ages to open. Now I've grown accustomed to the idiosyncrasies of this place. It's a tad strenuous, but one adapts.

I enter. Off go my broken K-mart work shoes. They are placed down neatly, somewhere near the shoe rack. I'd put them on the shoe rack, but there isn't enough room. Our shoes spill over, like the haphazardous aftermath of a stormy day.

I plod into my room and peel off my sticky socks. Then I throw my bag in the corner and change into some pyjamas. I pull on my fleeciest, warm ones.

Outside, the Jacarandas are blooming, littering the streets with their purple flowers. It's spring now, but nature hasn't gotten the memo. Or maybe my apartment is just really cold. I plod out of my room.

I find myself standing in the middle of the apartment, the living and dining areas blending.

What to do now?

I gravitate towards the kitchen. Even though it's one p.m., it's dark. James, my roommate, always pulls the blinds shut, and sometimes they remain like this for days. The shadows gather in the corner. If I wasn't paying enough attention, they would swallow me whole. Wrap me in dark tendrils and drag me into the earth. But they don't. They just glare at me, teasing and practically tangible. I divert my gaze and laboriously wind up the blinds. For a small amount of time I simply stand, simmering in the slight afternoon sun.

I flick the switch on the kettle. It pulsates with a dull orange glow. The machine is cheap and slow – but today I have time, if not money. I lean against the marble vinyl. It too is dark and peppered with crumbs. They stick to my arm and, one by one, I pick them off. They fall to the floor like little bready snowflakes.

The kettle squeals (despite being electrical) and eventually the timer clicks off. I pour the boiling water into my mug, letting the Bushells Blue Label seep. I check for milk. It goes off in two days, but I've only gotten a couple of cups out of it. Damn. What a waste.

I take my steaming mug of tea and wander back into the living / dining room. I spot my keyboard. Some piano on a Sunday afternoon could be lovely. I sleepily plug in headphones and begin to play.

First is *Mia and Sebastian's Theme* to warm up. It's slow and sad and poignant. Peter, my piano teacher, recommended it to me. It's from *La La Land* and he'd thought I would enjoy it.

'Girls like those kinds of movies,' he had said. I'd never seen it, and silently rejected his assumption that I'd like some airy-fairy romance musical. But then I watched it. And it was good.

I play it through once before moving onto the piece I'm learning – the *Moonlight Sonata*. I'm not very good at reading the music. I read it slowly, like a child reads a word.

'D ... O ... G ... Do ... Dog ... Oh that says dog!'

Mostly I just memorise the music, but to do that, one must go through the strenuous process of translation. Slowly, I read a note. Press the corresponding key. Then it gets put together in a more proper way.

Eventually there is something sounding like music. Playing becomes innate. It becomes a given. As if cotton candy, the music fills me with its sweet, coloured fluff.

But I don't play for very long. I drop onto the couch and watch something on TV. I couldn't say what I'm watching – it too is a type of fluff. It bulks my day with its irrelevance. There is something to be said for soapy distractions.

I'm waiting for James. He finishes work at five. After he is done, maybe we could do something fun – we could get dessert, or go out for drinks, or even just watch something a little more substantial than the suds I'm currently consuming.

So, I sit here, on the couch, until five rolls around.

Then I receive a stream of texts.

> *Going straight to Uni to work on project with Jayanna. Will let you know if it's a late dinner vibe or a go out or something. Idk yet depends on how quick we are.*
> *Either way*
> *It's drinkies night unless you have to work in the morning!*

But work is in the morning, so I send a sad reply and start to think about what to have for dinner.

I'm tired. Too tired to cook. So, I decide to chuck some frozen winter veggies into a bowl and microwave them. They spin round and round, injected with warmth as if on a cosy merry-go-round.

A few minutes elapse and I begin to eat. The food is only half thawed but I'll eat it anyway. I feel as though I'm devouring some odd sort of baby food, a weird cubic mush of orange, green and white. But it doesn't taste like mush, and it's important to eat, so the food is forced down.

I put the empty bowl in the sink.

Soon I tire. I'm left with nothing to do and crawl into the shadowed warmth of my bed. My window is open – the room filled with the same brilliant orange light of the morning. Only now it's later, much later. The sun falls asleep far too slowly during daylight savings. Like a bird in a cage, we have forced it to become a spectacle. To cover our blank, dark evenings. But now it flies off.

Under the sun's vermillion wing, I'm left wondering what I accomplished today. But I'm no longer filled with warm tea or fluffy, cotton candy feelings. Just the vague taste of mushy winter veggies when my teeth clicks against my tongue.

Death Kills

Sandra Joy

The first death I experienced was my own. That's a true story. The next death I experienced was my daddy's – and I killed him. That's almost a true story.

Although my mum was a London model, my dad was a farmer to the core. Hard work and long hours were all he ever knew, and I don't think I ever saw him in anything but moleskins, R.M. Williams boots, and his Akubra hat.

Dad's father had a sheep farm outside of Singleton. He wanted to raise cattle, but his bank manager friend convinced him that, 'the financial future of Australia is in sheep'. So, Pop invested in sheep – and went broke. Someone told me that he then changed banks and stopped buying the guy beer on Friday nights. Anyway, to get out of debt, Pop opened a shoe store at The Entrance. I have no idea how that transition of product, location and lifestyle came about; I just know it to be a crucial part of my existence.

I didn't get to meet my dad's parents, but I'd heard that my father was an only child and his mum apparently died when he was young so, not only was he close to his dad, but he was also the sole source of labour. As Dad grew, he worked on the farm (which was now growing lucerne and raising cattle) and he worked in the shoe store, travelling between the two as required. My dad was a hard worker.

It was in this shoe store that my parents met. It's a very romantic story (worthy of Hollywood) but it doesn't belong here. For now, just know that they met and had five children. Of these, the first two daughters married and turned my parents into grandparents. Their third child died at the tragic age of three days. After waiting a few years, they had two more children – my brother, Stuart, and another two years later, me.

Between all of this, Dad was finally able to buy his dream property. I don't know how many he looked at, but he narrowed it down to three and took Mum, Stuart and myself to help him make the final decision. Mum didn't like the one with the ugly house, but Stuart wanted its bike tracks. Dad and I both loved the one with the cottage and rose garden but, in the end, he chose Appletree Flat.

Our new home was a forty-minute drive northwest of Singleton, and the two hundred and fifty hectares of prime land was tucked into the base of the mountains of Wollemi National Park.

The property had everything Dad ever wanted: paddocks for lucerne and other crops, paddocks for cows and horses, sheds for machinery and hay bales, yards and pens for the chooks and pigs. It even had its own fuel tank, as well as two dams and a creek with a little bridge over it. I saw my first shooting star from that bridge.

My sisters had been into pony clubs and other horse activities, but times were different then. I didn't get to go riding often with my dad, but that's okay. I think that's why I treasure the few memories so much. Whenever we found the time to ride for pleasure, we'd take the horses to the top of a hill and just stop.

'So,' he'd start seriously, 'when you get married, we'll build you and your young man a house over under those trees, and you'll own all that area beyond that dam.'

'You are referring to the handsome guy who's going to move in just before I turn eighteen. Totally gorgeous, single and hard-working. The one from the perfect family.'

'Yeah, that's him,' he'd wink. 'And don't forget, ya mum will always expect you for Sunday lunch.'

'We'll be there. Kids 'n' all.'

Dad and I would banter for ages before moving on to the next range where we'd stop and map out another part of our future. It always involved me staying on the land and generations planting roots deep down on Appletree Flat.

As a teenager, I thought this place was perfect. I can only imagine how much my dad loved it.

What's more, to buy this land, he sold the two businesses he created and his other property. For the first time in three generations, this man – my dad – was debt free.

His life was good.

Then he got sick.

Over the next eighteen months, there were many days when Mum and Dad weren't there when I got home from school. They attended a lot of appointments, often travelling to Newcastle or Sydney (with or without us).

There was a sudden interest in vegetables and herbal medicine. Stuart and I both had to go on one of the trips to Sydney to see a naturopath. It was an eerie trip: for the first time ever, no-one was fighting. I read my book, Stuart played with something, and Mum wasn't yelling at Dad to slow down. I think they were preparing us for the disgusting medicine we went home with. Eeyoow! How do they get so much vile into such a small bottle!

The next day, Mum called Stuart and I into the kitchen before dinner and told us to sit down. There was no afternoon tea and no homework; the table was bare, so I was worried. Maybe they'd spent too much on Christmas and we had to forego our pocket-money for a while.

Dad was already sitting in his chair. He spent most of his time in that chair. I'm sure if I looked, it would be faded or dented beneath his mustard-coloured dressing-gown. Mum stood, leaning against the cupboard beside the stove. I could tell she was pretending not to cry. Neither of them looked at each other. This was bigger than pocket-money.

It was Mum who told us the details of the secret they'd been keeping for nearly two years. I don't remember her speaking, but I remember what she said. My dad had been diagnosed with sclerosis, emphysema, and asbestosis – a terminal combination of diseases that was causing him to suffer and deteriorate daily.

My dad was dying.

My daddy was going to die.

I looked across the table, but he didn't want to look at any of us. My breath had stopped and didn't re-emerge until my body overflowed with gasps for air mixed with bursts of tears. I couldn't stop the tears and I couldn't stop him from dying. This can't be true. This. Can't. Be. True.

Two weeks later, I started Year 10, but I hated being away from Dad. Because we lived so far from town, school days were seven a.m. to five p.m., and they seemed even longer.

In the second week of term we did a revision test. I knew I didn't want to be at school anymore, and Jenny bragging about beating me on that test was the final straw. I quit. I returned my textbooks to the supply room, emptied my locker, told my friends, and then told the lady at the office. She called the principal, and I spent over an hour convincing Sister Faith that I would not change my mind, but yes, I would consider coming back next year.

At last, she conceded that I had just unenrolled myself from high school and she asked how I would be getting home. I told her I would catch the bus to my sister's place, and she would drive me home in the morning. I also hoped the moral support would help when I told my parents.

'Okay then,' she offered, turning towards the window that revealed the lines of buses and students. 'Which bus?'

I looked over her shoulder and realised that neither of us had been watching the time. 'That one. The one that just left.'

Sister Faith drove me to my sister's house.

To be with Dad, I left school after doing only four weeks of year ten. I then spent my days at home on the farm. My sixteenth birthday was in February and no-one came. Jenny had a new boyfriend and the group had plans. The textbooks don't warn you that having a dying father makes you a leper. So, I sat in my bedroom listening to the song, 'It's My Party' by Lesley Gore. You probably know it: 'It's my party and I'll cry if I want to; you would cry too if it happened to you'. I played it on repeat and ate chocolate cake by myself.

When I left my room to get more cake, Dad was back in his chair at the kitchen table. He must have just taken his medication because his breathing was still very deep and loud. I knew this embarrassed him, so I decided that I'd had enough cake, and slipped back to my bedroom without him noticing.

Dad and I spent a lot of time together. One day, when he was still able to drive, he wanted to buy some things from Maitland. I was in the back seat with the windows down, watching and listening. He and the salesman were at the back of the car and Dad was stuttering and stammering, trying to ask for the tractor part the farm needed. The young salesman was so impatient and rude, mocking Dad for his inability to articulate. I wanted to jump out and hit him! I wanted to yell at that idiot and tell him to be nice because that was my daddy and he is dying. But I was polite. Instead, I got out and walked to the back of the station wagon and told him what Dad needed. From that day on, I became Dad's spokesperson.

For some reason, I was the one person who could understand him. I don't know if I was more determined, or just had better interpretation skills, but nobody was going to insult my father like that again.

On the 2nd of June 1983, we were driving home from Singleton: Mum and Dad in the front, Stuart and I in the back. I don't even know what my brother and I were debating, but I remember Mum turning around and telling me to shut up. Not Stuart. Just me. And it hurt. Worse still, later I was proven to be right (in whatever the dispute was about).

For me, at that time, it was another last straw. Once again, Stuart was the favoured child and, once again, I was disregarded. As soon as we got home, he headed down to the caravan to be with his future wife, Heather. I headed to my bedroom and listened to 'Solid Rock' by Goanna.

Then, for some overwhelming reason, I went to my dad's medicine cupboard in the kitchen and took his packet of Serapax. I knew that Dad needed these, but I didn't think of that at the time. *I'm so sorry, Dad.*

I went back to the solitude of my bedroom with one thought in my mind – would anyone care if I died? It wasn't that I wanted to kill myself, I just wanted to know how they would react when they thought I was dead. I wanted to know if they would miss me?

Looking back now, I obviously wasn't thinking clearly or maturely. After all, Dad not having his pills could have killed him and, if taking his pills killed me, I wouldn't be able to see anyone's reaction anyway. But that didn't stop me. I swallowed thirty-one of them.

Heather came into my room unannounced, as she often did. Stuart probably sent her to check on me; sometimes he was nice. She sat on the bed and looked at me, then saw the bottle in my hand. She jumped up and demanded, 'What have you done?'

By this stage I was quite calm (probably sedated) and so I told her: 'I've just taken thirty-one.' Then the thought of getting into trouble entered my mind and I quickly added, 'But please don't tell anyone.'

So ... she didn't.

She went back to the caravan. Back to Stuart.

A short time later, a horrible taste with a hot foam made its way up my throat and I called out to Mum. She panicked and asked the same question.

'I've taken thirty-one of these and I think the coating has come off 'cos it tastes horrible.'

I don't know what she did next, but my brother soon laid me in the back seat of his car and raced me to Singleton Hospital. Apparently, he was pulled over for speeding, but when he explained, the police gave him a lights-and-sirens escort to the hospital. I wish I had seen that, but by the time we arrived, I was clinically dead. They were able to revive me (obviously) and I spent the next seven days in a coma.

I'd never heard of a catheter so, when I finally woke up, I wondered why I didn't have to wee. I laid awake for some time before getting the nurse's attention, watching the monitors and wondering if I was wetting myself. Maybe I had broken that part of me and so I didn't need to wee anymore.

Mum and Stuart visited, so did my sisters and their families, but Dad was too sick to travel. Did he run out of tablets because of me? Was he stressed out worrying about *me*? Were Mum and Dad blaming themselves, or each other, for what *I* did?

Dad was now too sick to travel and that's my fault.

So, when the doctor told me that I couldn't go straight home, that they had decided to send me to a psychiatric facility, I was determined to change their mind and get home to my daddy. Before the psychiatrist appeared for his final assessment, I had worked out what he wanted to hear: 'No, I'll never do it again.'

After two weeks in hospital, and a few days of saying the right thing, they gave me permission to go home. Mum had to go to the office to sign the paperwork and collect my belongings. She came back into the ward and explained that they had needed to cut up my clothes to gain immediate access to my chest, so they were no good. I fought back the tears over my favourite Johnny Cougar t-shirt, but I was in no position to complain. I couldn't remember what else I had been wearing.

Mum then held up a plastic bag with my 24 silver bracelets, leather and silver necklaces and eight silver rings. 'And the lady at the office said to me,' Mum grinned, 'Would you please buy your daughter a jewellery box so she can leave some of it at home.'

I still laugh whenever I put on jewellery.

Because of his breathing difficulties, Dad spent his nights propped up on the kitchen table, trying to sleep. Until that night.

Exactly one month after my overdose, Dad went to bed for the first time in months. In the early hours of the morning, Mum tried to roll him over because he was hogging her side. He wouldn't move. He couldn't move. My dad was dead. I overdosed on the second of June 1983 and on the second of July 1983 my daddy died. That coincidence haunted me for years. Would he have lived longer if I didn't overdose? I was in a coma for a week, in hospital for a fortnight, but I blamed myself for years that the stress of my actions shortened my dad's life. How much longer would he have been with us if I hadn't been so selfish?

I regressed. My mind wandered back to the period when Dad travelled a lot for his business. I subconsciously told myself that he was away fitting out someone's kitchen, or at a rodeo or getting supplies for the shop. I struggled to accept that my daddy wasn't coming home. Ever. Maybe this was my age, or maybe it was the only way I could cope with the guilt that he'd still be alive if I hadn't been so stupid and selfish. Sometimes I still think that, but mostly now I know it's not true.

At his funeral, my crying became uncontrollable when they lowered his coffin into the ground. With my new thinking that he was only away, I couldn't comprehend the funeral and my conscious mind fought back, 'They can't do that to my daddy!'

But they did, and my brother-in-law carried my failing body to the car. Which car? No idea. A car. The car. I didn't care. I wanted my daddy. *I'm so sorry Daddy. I'm so sorry for causing you to die.*

Home

Kate Mannell

Home means different things to different people. It can be peaceful and familiar. It can be suffocating. It's a place that can hold the heart, and a place that can break the heart. Its essence can manifest in many places, or sometimes only the one.

The fan hummed and wobbled loosely in the popcorned ceiling finish that reminded me of cheap motel rooms. Mr McPhillamy, whom all the other girls referred to as Mr Mac, paced the matted navy carpet and tried to elicit interest in coral bleaching of the Great Barrier Reef.

I browsed the hike to Machu Picchu on my laptop, scrunching my face in disgust upon reading about people losing their toenails when climbing Dead Woman's Pass – the highest point of the Inka Trail.

On my final night in Bathurst, I had to work the afternoon shift at the Coles deli. The supermarket had been my life during my final years of high school and the few months since graduation. Friendships, romances, and dramas had all played out inside, and outside, the old Coles' concrete walls. I'd toilet-papered the cars of my friends in the carpark outside the back door, and chanted catchy tunes over the loudspeaker to sell roast chickens. Even staged a fake fight with a mate, just to stir gossip throughout the store.

No one said goodbye as I clocked off that night. Many had already left before me.

Every set of lights stayed green for me as I drove out of town, passing them in a silent farewell I had thought would never come. The warm February air blew through my open windows, and I breathed in deeply the fresh country air as I sped down the highway faster than my red P-plates permitted.

It took two weeks for reality to hit. There was a girl my age in the tour group who had made comments about how envious she was of my carefree attitude, while she was battling with homesickness. I'd stood at the base of Christ the Redeemer, gotten drunk on Caipirinhas while cruising the bay of Paraty, and floated down a river in Brotas on an inflatable ring.

How could Bathurst be better than this?

When I first heard my mother's voice after that two weeks, I began to sob. It never fully occurred to me that I would not see her for four months – that I'd really be away … for four months.

I'd dated a boy a couple of years before high school ended. He was sweet and gentle and loved to listen to country music. All my friends seemed to like the genre, but the sound made me cringe. After breaking up with that boy, the music reminded me too much of his small red car and dreams that revolved around me. He had decided not to go for a job because he didn't want to be away from me. I decided I didn't want to be the reason for his lack of ambition.

I had been almost two months away from home. The tour was nearing the southernmost town on Earth, with the icy desolation to prove it. The days on the truck were long as we covered thousands of kilometres, only stopping to eat and sleep by the side of the road.

It was those days, feeling as isolated and forsaken as the Patagonian steppe that stretched unfettered towards the horizon, lost in my own thoughts, I decided to play the songs I had so vehemently refused to listen to. I found they told stories of the simple and intimate kind; the stories that mended and widened the cracks in my heart. They reminded me of nights around bonfires or driving down highways with the windows down. Of the changing seasons, summer rains and taking the path to home.

The boring hometown I'd left behind suddenly began to change. I now missed the towering poplar trees that had marked every season of my life with their brilliant leaf cycles of colour, barrenness, and growth. I yearned for the steaming aromatic baths and flickering candles, that were perfected by an accompaniment of gentle rain falling in the soft, grey light outside. The familiar main street of town, sharp winter breeze through the park, homecooked meals, and family get-togethers. The gathering of neighbours on the wooden verandah, wine glasses in hands, to toast a full moon rising over the hills speckled with cattle.

Trekking helped me make sense of it all.

In the small town of El Chalten, I went on my first solo trek. Soft pinks and oranges painted the sky, and cast a hazy light on the dirt trail and the trees along it – as I set out on the trail early in the morning. In places, the path was exhausting and painful. In others, exhilarating and beautiful. It is the attitude you maintain that shapes the trek.

Seventy-nine days after I left home, I arrived at the Sun Gate. It had taken three chilly nights camping at high altitudes, and four days of walking, to arrive. As

I paused to catch my breath, the clouds parted to reveal the glory of Machu Picchu perched upon the mountain top. All day, heavy mists, rain, and brief moments of clarity rotated like clockwork through the ancient ruins. My nose was burnt and blistered by the sun and the cold, but I had kept all my toenails intact.

A small TV on the wall quietly showed *The Man in the Iron Mask* in Spanish as I gorged on a deliciously creamy alfredo pasta, while the mighty Urubamba River swelled outside from the constant rain. The warmth in my stomach radiated to my aching bones. I couldn't have been more content. The eight of us who had elected to walk the Inka Trail, rested in the quiet restaurant, stranded in the small town of Aguas Calientes until the train would take us back to Cusco.

The year before I left home, I'd ripped a page from a magazine and blu-tacked it to my wall. A quote in bold writing over a photo of Machu Picchu read, 'there are two times in life, now and too late'.

On my final night in South America, after a dreamy couple of days at an ecolodge in the Amazon, I was packing my bags for the final time. The past few months had been wonderful and agonising. I'd wake on the cusp of consciousness, thinking the morning birds were singing, and the golden sunlight was rising over the valley at home, only to find myself alone in a dark tent on cold ground. Gazing into the lush equatorial jungles along the roadsides, I would close my eyes and see grassy paddocks and tall eucalypts instead.

Waves crashed onto the beach I'd spent my childhood summers visiting. It felt odd to be there in the off-season, when the cicadas had stopped their song and disappeared underground. Wrapped in my alpaca shawl, I felt lost as I stared out across the Pacific towards the land I'd just returned from. Distant sprays of white water could be seen in the deep blue ocean, marking the location of whales beneath the sparkling surface as they journey on their migration. My mother and grandmother sat beside me, anchoring me against the fresh winter wind while the spouts of water moved further up the coast.

Another four months passed before I was ready to escape again. By placing ID tags in books at the quiet library, I'd managed to save enough for a two-week trip to another land. The airport's departure gates welcomed me back, dissolving the remnant threads of fear that no longer held power over me. On arrival, a chorus of blaring horns filled the air while an intoxicating mix of spice, incense and waste assaulted my nose. Culture shock set in. I loved every moment.

The turquoise glacial water of the Ganges swirled beside us as our large raft bounced along on the rapids. When the dips in the water became more intense and monstrous waves rose before the raft, we squealed and grasped the handholds for dear life. In a less dangerous section of rapids, some of us dived into the cool and refreshing water, marvelling at its strength in pulling our floating bodies along with the current.

I blissfully immersed myself in the water straight from the Himalayas, soaking in its vibrant life force. Reaching the end of our run, the others struggled to pull my dead weight back into the raft as I laughed so much I could barely breathe. Doug from Australia jokingly described me as a 'wet, flopping seal'.

The setting sun reflected like molten copper onto the vivid blue waves, shimmering just beyond the rapids, before disappearing behind hazy mountains. That night, by the fire, our rafting guide recounted tales of tigers, campsite paw prints and missing dogs. The dreadlocked Canadian stared into the dancing flames with glazed eyes. I lost my appetite when he mentioned the bodies that were floating in the river during our rafting. One wedged in between the rocks not far from where I'd dived into the river.

The plan was always university. I procrastinated, but eventually decided it was a safer option than waiting around for something better. From the time I was old enough to understand, I was certain I wanted to leave Bathurst. While I never imagined exactly where I'd end up, I was sure it would *not* be there. My undergraduate degree lasted three years. For two years I loved Newcastle, finding that coastal, progressive, big-town-but-not-city vibe perfect for me.

But then it came back.

The yearning for the rolling hills and creek-side eucalypts. The icy winter winds. The moon rises over the valley. What I thought was just a reaction to overseas culture shock revealed itself to be a seemingly perpetual condition.

The problem was, I had a home in Newcastle now too. And what if I were to return to Bathurst, only to tire of it as I did in high school? What if I were to ache for the late-night visits to the breakwall – cast in a sickly lamp light while dark waves crashed against it – or the screeching rainbow lorikeets in the angophoras, or the lush green flood plains spotted with cows and herons?

It was time for morning tea, so we drifted towards the shade cast by a line of lichen-streaked casuarinas while the wind whispered through their needle-like leaves. Tying the rope mooring line loosely around a branch, Leigh sat at the bow and threw his banana peel into the water. The AM radio crackled in the background as we discussed mosquitoes and the cricket. On this first day of paid work in my field, I wondered what path my life would take.

I left pieces of myself across the world. Part of me remains with the thundering falls of Iguazu, in the crystal-clear waters of the Rio Bonito. There are traces of me scattered across the desolate plains of the harsh Patagonian steppe and through the Andes mountains. In polluted streets of buzzing New Delhi, and the flickering candles of incense-filled temples in the Himalayan mountains. I exist in the paddocks of the central west region of New South Wales, and the gently flowing creeks beneath eucalypt shade. Along the buzzing Honeysuckle harbourside city track and mosquito infested university campus.

Home is where the heart is. This heart is in too many places.

I find the thought both comforting and confronting that this story will grow with age. More homes will be formed, some even lost, along the way. While it was only a few years ago, I wish I could return and ask myself how I was so sure. I've asked so many around me how they knew where to call home. The answers rarely inspire. With borders closed in response to a threatening virus, there is no escape to be that girl whose wanderlust helped gain perspective.

Sitting with a friend on a rainy Monday, we played Mario Kart, as we did when we were young neighbours, and discussed our plans. We'd both left the rolling hills to study by the sea. He quoted to me Robert Frost, as I pondered my dilemma of which path to take.

> Two roads diverged in a yellow wood,
> And sorry I could not travel both
> And be one traveller, long I stood
> And looked down one as far as I could
> To where it bent in the undergrowth.

I didn't need to hear the rest to know, I had to take the path that would lead me home. But the question persists, where is home?

The answer remains unwritten.

Sweet Tooth

Lucy Egan

Butterscotch 'sponge' pudding

Prep time: 15 min
Setting time: 2 hrs
Serves: 4-6

80g butter
3 eggs, separated
1 cup milk
¼ cup water
3 tsp gelatine powder

1. Melt the butter and sugar in a saucepan, then transfer to a mixing bowl and set aside to cool slightly. Whisk in the egg yolks, then gradually the milk, whisking constantly (but not vigorously).
2. Put water in small bowl and sprinkle the gelatine over. Stand a minute to soften, then either microwave for 30 seconds or stand the bowl in a pan of hot water, whisking with a fork until the gelatine has dissolved and the mixture is clear. Cool slightly and then stir in milk mixture.
3. Refrigerate for 10 mins, stirring occasionally, until thickened slightly (take care not to leave it too long).
4. Use electric beaters to beat egg whites to soft peaks. Fold into milk mixture and pour into 6-capacity serving dish. Refrigerate for 2 hours until set.
5. Spoon into bowls and serve with fruit and ice-cream.

Butterscotch pudding

Mum talks about my grandma's cooking a lot. Something that sticks in her mind, aside from the three-course breakfasts they used to sit down to every morning until she was sixteen, was this butterscotch pudding. This wobbly and soft, melt-in-your-mouth butterscotch pudding. She always sounds very nostalgic and romantic when she describes it. My mum is not a sweet tooth.

Ingredients:
1 cup brown sugar, 2 eggs, 2 cups milk, 2 tablespoons plain flour, 2 tablespoons butter

Recently, she returned to her hometown of Inverell in country northern NSW to visit her mum; or, as me and my sister call her, Barndy. (This nickname arises from my inability to say Grandy – her preferred name – when I was little, and it stuck). It's a seven-hour drive from Newcastle and Barndy lives alone on her property, with her cattle, and her dog and cat for company.

Mix flour and sugar, add beaten yolks and milk gradually

Mum has lived in Newcastle for twenty-two years now, after moving for my dad's job shortly after I was born. Her heart has always belonged to where she grew up. It's a place of big blue skies, long yellow grass, swaying eucalypts, red-brown soil, utes, kangaroos, dams, gullies, delicate wildflowers, Chinese restaurants, churches, and animals – both domesticated and wild.

Put on boil and thicken whilst stirring

Now Barndy is older, we like to return the favour of cooking for her. She used to cook for us when we were younger and we would visit nearly every holiday. Mum's dad was a pig farmer. Barndy fed, cleaned and looked after the girls and the house, while Old John fed, cleaned and looked after the pigs and the piggery. Barndy was used to cooking for her four daughters, their husbands and her seven grandchildren.

Add butter and put in buttered pie dish

My sister and I are vegetarian. I have been my whole life. Barndy tackled the challenge admirably and would cook us boiled or roasted veges with rice, crumbed fish, and a handful of nuts for protein. She had a knack for choosing the best mangoes, tomatoes and avocados in season. We never said anything because we understood that it was a big deal to ask our grandma to supply us with food for something that was a conscious choice. We knew from a young age that it wasn't really fair to expect someone who grew up in the Great Depression to exclude a whole food group, even if it was because I just genuinely never liked meat. Later, she cooked mac and cheese because she knew we liked it.

Beat egg whites with ½ cup of sugar

She cooked the best cakes and slices. I always looked forward to holidays (both Lai and my birthdays fell in the school holidays) if we were going to Inverell because Barndy cooked us cakes and sweets.

She cooked a Cadbury chocolate cake off the back of the packet and my sister loved her pumpkin fruit cake. She cooked for us all when we went to pony camp and had to provide morning tea. Barndy was a member of the CWA (Country Women's Association) and often participated in the bake sales that entailed. She always worried that her cooking wasn't good enough, that it was undercooked or imperfect, but we always loved it.

Bake in oven until meringue is nicely brown

Mum thought it would be nice to cook Barndy the butterscotch pudding that stuck in her own mind so much.

We had a recipe from Merle's Kitchen, a cookbook written by the older lady from MasterChef a few years ago. She was also a member of the CWA and was famed for her older style recipes like cakes, biscuits and slices.

Mum gathered all the ingredients together in Newcastle and then trekked up to Inverell. Mum, like Barndy, also worries about the quality of her cooking. She followed the instructions in the recipe (see the top of the first page) but for some reason, the pudding didn't set properly.

Barndy ate it anyway. She ate most of it. Mum was very apologetic and was still teary about it a few days later. She couldn't understand why it hadn't worked out and felt that it was confirmation of her poor cooking skills.

They discussed the fallibility of recipes and Barndy said she enjoyed it anyway. She offered Mum her original, old CWA recipe book to give to me (I also love cooking sweets and desserts). It's beautiful, with thin brown pages stamped with careful lettering and simple recipes, splashed with chocolate and flour from years of use.

I think of Barndy poring over this cookbook, cooking furiously for her family of four girls and Old John and later, the CWA. I can feel the deliberate act of caring for someone else, of nurturing them with food. Of opening yourself up to change and criticism. The magic of transforming one thing into another. And then years later, Mum committing the same act of love, for us and for Barndy. Barndy knew that. She understood that.

The way to our family's heart is through our stomachs.

Sonder

Clarissa Chawner

It's strange for me to think that my parents had a life before they had children. The photo taken on the day they got married has always sat on top of the piano, in every house we've lived in. The frame is plain silver. Tarnished. Mum and Dad look so young. Less wrinkles, more hair, in Dad's case. I remember reading somewhere that, to be a good parent, you need to have this innate ability to *give*. I don't think I'd make a good parent. I'm selfish. I'm bad at sharing, even though I have a younger brother.

I don't think I could ever use the word selfish to describe my parents. The older I get, the more grateful I am for everything my parents have done to set me up for a successful life. From forcing timid, eleven-year-old me to order my own meals at restaurants, to buying my first car with money they'd saved.

Mum has always been, and will hopefully always be, a phone call away. She is always there to listen, console or advise. Dad, when he picks up – he's notoriously bad at answering the phone – is there as well, always with a terrible pun.

Dad loves to say that he and Mum met through tragedy. Mum rolls her eyes at this, but she'll smile at the same time. Dad always manages to get a laugh out of her, even if it's an exasperated one. Dad lived in the barracks of Townsville's army base when he and Mum first met. Apparently, Mum and her aunt had come on base to catch up with some friends of Mum's cousin, Troy, who drowned a few months earlier. Dad and Troy knew each other, somehow.

I can imagine Mum surrounded by all these fit young army guys, and choosing Dad. I can definitely see Dad being charming when he was younger. Awkwardly charming, but charming nonetheless. He's the type of person that laughs at his own jokes, and you can't help but laugh as well.

In one of our regular phone calls, I was complaining to Mum about my roommates' inability to do the washing-up. As I was lamenting about the piles of dirty dishes, I could hear Dad laughing in the background.

'It's a rite of passage that everyone goes through, sweet,' Mum says matter-of-factly. 'You complain about them now. Just wait until you move in with Jacob. Then you'll be complaining about him.'

'Not like us!' chimes in Dad. 'Thirty years of domestic bliss, isn't that right, honey?'

'Yes,' Mum says dryly. 'Domestic bliss.'

'Exactly! Did I ever tell you about Corey, Clarissa?' Dad asks.

He then regales me with tales of the first place he and Mum lived together. It was a share-house in Townsville. Mum, Dad and three other housemates – one of which was the infamous Corey. Apparently, Corey never washed up. Ever. It drove Mum mad. Once, Corey left a frying pan to 'soak' on the stove for several days, until Mum couldn't take it anymore. She confronted him, and he denied everything.

I can't decide if, at my age, Mum would have had less or more of a temper than she does now. As time goes on, she uses the words that shouldn't be repeated around polite company with increasing regularity. Maybe she was more forgiving when she was younger. Still, I can imagine Dad begging Mum to let it go, then Mum braining poor, unsuspecting Corey over the head with the frying pan.

According to Mum, Dad did a lot of dumb things when he was younger. I can definitely believe this, because he still does dumb things now. From car accidents in sugarcane drainage-ditches, to run-ins with the axe when chopping wood.

One memorable story I've been told is of a hydraulic hose coming loose and whacking Dad in the head, cutting a huge gash in his forehead. Mum says he walked into the house with his hand on his head and asked, 'does this look bad?'. When he moved his hand, a huge flap of bloody skin flopped over his eyes.

Dad at his finest, truly.

Despite everything, they made it through a few years of dating, another few years of engagement, and finally to marriage.

To be honest, Mum and Dad's wedding kind of seemed like a shemozzle, although Mum speaks of it with fondness. They had a small, intimate wedding on a Sunday, with forty-five guests. It was only marred by the fact that Mum and Dad found out ten days beforehand, that Dad was going to be deployed overseas on an army operation. For four months. Dad didn't even have the pleasure of telling Mum this himself. They both found out over the radio.

Consequently, they didn't get a honeymoon. Apparently, they had already booked – and paid for – a two-week cruise in the Whitsundays. The company was kind enough to refund them, thankfully.

Plus, they also almost had a car accident on the way to the reception. Dad's twin brother, Uncle Darren, was driving. To quote Mum, 'he almost got us collected at an intersection two hours after the wedding'.

A few years after the wedding, Dad's second in command, Brad Murtagh, who was a part of the wedding party, died of bone cancer.

On a high-school excursion to Sydney, Mum was one of the accompanying parents. During our daytrip to the Museum of Human Disease, I distinctly remember hearing about Mum bursting into tears in front of a cross-section of a leg. She had to be ushered outside and comforted by the English teacher. Only later did I learn that whoever was attached to that leg in life, had died of bone cancer.

It's moments like these that I realise that my parents have rich life histories, full of people that I've only ever heard about in stories, whose faces I'll only ever see in photos.

I've always found it overwhelming, when I walk into other people's houses and they have multitudes of family photos on every surface. Instead, we have the dozens of photo albums lined up on the bottom of the bookshelf, and a select few photos in a place of pride on top of the piano. They've gone through several rotations over the years. But the one that's always there, is the picture of my parents on their wedding day.

Lineage

Charlotte Rae

To be born, you need two parents. You also need four grandparents, eight great grandparents, sixteen great, great grandparents, and so on and so forth until you're left with a fathomless lineage of ancestors who all had to be born and meet at just the right time and place for you to eventually arrive so miraculously and surely right where you are: alive.

Perhaps that is a bit of a selfish thing to think about as you look at a picture of your parents taken long before you were born – back when they had smooth skin and white smiles and didn't even know you – but I think about it. And the very thought of all those gossamer chances and inexplicable fates tied together through the generations to eventually create me, leaves me trembling in a fearful, reverent gratitude.

What if one single action of any single person down the line had been different?

Behind the smiles, the teeth, the curves of face, and the eye colours of my beaming parents in this photograph is so much more than just atoms and cells. Behind those faces lie a sprawling descent of loves and losses, choices and mistakes, ocean waves and a cascading swirl of generations, reaching back through a millennium. This picture contains two pasts of incomprehensible complexity entwining and finding one another in crisp blue uniforms with me, twinkling in their eyes.

My mother's ancestry extends back into a time of convicts – petty criminals from Ireland and Scotland shipped to Australia for life. Toiling and meeting and falling in love around the evolving nation until my great grandparents ended up settled in this tiny country town that is still my home.

Look closely at the family tree and you'll see my first great uncle was born seven months after my great grandmother was married – a strapping, full-sized baby. I've never heard a single mention of this little anomaly, but I must confess it rather looks like the modern Macpherson dynasty was born when Minnie Dorothea jumped the broom.

Later on, my grandma always considered herself the belle of her huge family. Wildly flirtatious, she would compete with her sisters about who could kiss the most men at a dance before the night was out. But she swore on her life she would never marry a hairy man or a butcher. One day when she was fourteen, she saw Jack playing tennis and said to herself right then and there she would marry him. I guess – luckily for me – she had no way of knowing back then that he would turn out to be both a hairy man *and* a butcher.

Mum was the youngest of seven siblings: an argument won by my grandma who wanted one more baby. She grew up riding horses around her country town with a string of beaux at her heel. She wanted to start an Appaloosa stud when she grew up, until this dream begat that of being a glamorous flight attendant. But she didn't get the job. Instead, she decided out of the fated blue to become a policewoman. It was one morning as she sat in her childhood home flicking through a careers book that she called out to her mother,

'Mum, I think I'll be a policewoman.'

'All right, dear' my grandma replied, and continued to wash the dishes.

On my father's side is a history of quieter people and fewer numbers. There are no secret convicts or mad women in his lineage. Rather, my granddad's family had immigrated here from the misty wilds of Scotland in the early twentieth century. But why did they choose this mysterious, sunburned nation? When they had to leave their storied homeland, Granddad's uncles chose to settle in Canada and the United States, the other side of the world to where I am now.

Born a month earlier than Mum to a little family of just three boys, my father grew up in a suburban home an hour away. He left school to become an electrician, and later a soldier. He had wanted to join the Air Force but couldn't get in; Dad has often told me he'd probably still be there now if he had – an old bachelor Flight Officer. In any case, after nine years that didn't take him into Afghanistan, he swapped his green camouflage for a blue uniform at the Police Academy – where Mum was now an instructor.

Mum had countless boyfriends through the years, even an engagement somewhere along the line, but Dad swears he never went on a single date until he met her (despite, he tells me, all the women who had thrown himself at his feet for a decade on account of his blue eyes and ripped chest.) The first time she met him, Mum could barely look past the most hideous knitted jumper she had ever seen. But I suppose the intrigue of meeting someone whose last name was the same as her middle name won out against the cacophonous colours of the wool. Dad could hardly look past the fact she inexplicably sprinkled the word "ciao" through her conversations. Nonetheless, it was a matter of weeks before they were quite in love.

My mother became Meredyth Rae Rae and I ended up here – thanking every lucky star and tennis match, unaccountable decision and unavoidable failure, destined chance, and lucky meeting that all conspired to find me right where I am: alive.

Herstory

Rewriting female family history and my story

Lucy Egan

My sister and I grew up on a diet of Mum's family stories. She grew up on a farm, in a family of four sisters. Her dad was a pig farmer and her mum, a homemaker. She told us about the land, the animals, her large extended family – most of whom still lived around her hometown of Inverell. I loved these stories and could never get enough.

I would often force my dad to tell me stories as I went to bed, of his and Mum's time in Moree, which we left not long after I was born. I would force him to trace patterns on my back and tell me stories about the arid and hot-blooded town. Mum's family has a very strong identity and rich familial mythology. It is matriarchal, with my grandma the head of the family. Mum and her sisters lost their dad, Old John, around the age I am now. For most of my life, we migrated to Inverell every second Christmas to have it as a whole family at Barndy's house and property, with the other sisters and their husbands and children.

Mum's family presence was a very strong influence in my life. I adored my aunties and loved different parts about all of them. I had less to do with my dad's family; we saw them for birthdays and Christmases – but it was complicated. The Morse family was a family of loud, smart, sporty, laughing, and strong girls. I wanted to be one of them.

Mum bought a subscription to *Ancestry* in preparation for our first big family European trip in 2017. I was one year out of high school and enrolled in vet nursing one day a week at TAFE. I had always loved Mum's family stories and loved the idea of finding out secrets, dramas, records, and stories. I was lost and uncertain of my future, of myself.

In high school, when we had free computer time, I would get on *Ancestry* and play with my family tree, as much as the free version would allow.

When Mum asked me to help her trace back some of her heritage so we could visit some of these mythical places, places where our ancestors lived and loved before us, I was excited. More stories to add to my growing collection and add to my concept of myself, shaken by adolescence, trauma, and uncertainty.

I loved *Ancestry* and being able to access all these different records, and discover aspects of the family previously unknown by us, and by my grandma. Within Mum's family there was a strong focus on preserving family history, with my Aunt Trish chasing up the Morse side, my mum recording stories about her adventurer cousin Stafford, and my grandpa's siblings holding onto family documents. The men had military records, as well as travelling records and census records, careers and business identities.

I was fascinated by the women. I knew from my mum's stories about my family that I came from a line of matriarchs, mothers, wives, daughters, academics, sisters, travellers, and homemakers. But most of the records on *Ancestry* focussed on the birth, marriage, children, and death of the women in my family. There was a lot of negative space to fill in with stories, dreams and ideas. I could smell stories, and craved more than the two-dimensional depictions allowed by government bureaucracy and the wormhole of *Ancestry*.

I loved Great-aunt Mary – who was an avid world traveller, librarian, cat mum and French speaker – who died from cancer when I was eight. I loved to hear about Barndy as a young woman, who rode horses, went to boarding school, survived the Great Depression and WWII, and married Old John for love. I wanted to know more about my mum's Granny, who was small and posh. I wanted to know about mum's Great-aunt Em, who left Australia in the fifties for England. I wanted to hear about Old John's sisters and the wives of Old John's brothers, these amazing people who lived full and interesting lives. I never got tired of hearing about Mum and her sisters' travels, their education, their stops and starts in life.

Great-aunt Em, born in 1894, apparently decided she couldn't cope in Australia's social scene in the late 1950s and emigrated to England to live there for the rest of her life. She was an enigma in Mum's family. She wrote letters to my grandma, but my grandma couldn't remember where she lived or died, except that it was in Cornwall. Mum didn't remember either, except that she died in 1996, when Mum was married and teaching in Moree with Dad – a world away. Aunt Em was a Rothe, descended from Waldemar Henrik who came to Australia in 1871. Mum was determined to visit her grave and pay her respects to this strong, independent woman, who used to send them little presents. She very clearly remembers meeting her on Aunt Em's last visit to Australia in 1979 when she was little.

Ancestry did not yield any answers about where she was, except that she died in a retirement village in Mary Tavy. After a few weeks of frustrating dead-ends, I ended up googling her full name, Emmeline Frances Rothe. A newspaper notice with the details of the solicitors responsible for executing her will came up. With nothing to lose, I emailed the solicitors, enquiring if they had any records of Great-aunt Em. Because it was twenty years after she died, they were only able to give us the name of the funeral directors. Determined, and enjoying the creation of another story, I emailed the funeral directors. A week or so later, they emailed back with her grave's location!

On a grey day, we drove to the village of Whitchurch and saw the stark stone grave surrounded by pine trees, older crumbling graves, and a small church. Mum left supermarket flowers and I left an Australian $2 coin on the grave. It was just after Christmas and decorations were still up in the tiny church. The minister organised for Mum and Dad to meet with someone who knew Aunt Em. She said Aunt Em was a small lady who could barely be seen above the wheel of her yellow Morris Minor and was associated with the church but didn't attend it.

These small details etched a hazy mirage of Aunt Em, but I loved her anyway, even if it was just an idea of her. I was in awe of this mysterious lady who left everything she knew to live and die alone, aged 102, in a foreign country.

When we got home, we drove six hours to the country to tell my grandma and show her photos. She exclaimed, "Ah I remember where she was now! I remember sending letters to Whitchurch!".

Aunt Em wasn't the only adventurer and explorer in the family. My grandma's sister, my Great-aunt Mary, was also an avid and extensive solo world traveller in a time where women were encouraged to settle down and marry. She visited Spain, the UK, USA, Peru, Thailand, Romania, Russia, Germany, French Polynesia, Chile, Japan, Bulgaria, Morocco, Jordan, Egypt, France, Portugal, Finland, Vietnam, Hong Kong, Argentina, Canada, Turkey, Poland, Czech Republic, Slovenia, Greece, Macedonia, Denmark, Malaysia, and Burma. That's what I can gather from her passports anyway. Mary travelled alone in tour groups.

I knew Mary when I was little. She was small, had big owlish glasses, short brown hair, and a kind voice. She had a little white flat in Mosman with two black and white cats named Honore and Henry – after the French composers. I loved Mary. She died in 2006. Mum and Dad sorted her flat afterwards. I ended up with her opera furs and a jade egg. Mum and I used to imagine her with the furs on, going to a French or Russian opera, mysterious lover by her side. We also ended up with some of her geisha paintings, a fuchsia flower in a pot, classical records, a cubist still life, two antique wooden armchairs, a big mirror, and her car. Mum drove her 1999 Toyota Corolla for years, until 2018 when she needed to get a bigger car and Mo (short for Mozart, one of Mary's favourite composers) was too old.

Around the time we were looking at going to Europe and chasing the final resting place of Great-aunt Em, Mum unearthed Mary's passports. Barndy was turning eighty that year and we were making a big present because we weren't going to be there for the party.

I poured over Mary's four passports for a morning, deciphering the stamps of all the countries she visited, translating them into a timeline and a map for

Barndy. I even fantasised about visiting all the places Mary went and writing about it, retracing her steps all those years later.

I still do.

Barndy tells stories about Mary being the cheeky, younger sister. She used to read books in the bath and when she was getting dressed. I do that too. It seemed as though Mary was reaching out to me, saying it was okay to be by myself, and study, and love books, and travel. Recently, Mum gave me her passports to keep. I keep them with Barndy's CWA cookbook.

Mum and I think of Mary whenever we see a rainbow. I love rainbows anyway; I think they are a small wonder in the everyday of our lives. On the trip in which Mary travelled for the last time, we saw multiple rainbows on the freeway. It was grey and dark, but there was occasionally a patch of sun and an arc of a rainbow winging across the sky, all the way home. Mum said it was Mary. I still think of her every time I see one and it reminds me to be myself, as Mary was.

My grandma is one of the strongest people I know. She is eighty-two, still living on her property in Inverell, and has lived twelve years without her sister and twenty-six without her husband. Mum's older sister, Kate, lives there too, about fifteen minutes' drive away. Barndy still runs a small mob of cattle who have calves every year. She adores her calves.

Animals are a love language for Barndy. Mum tells many stories of the pets they had growing up, a virtual menagerie. Barndy will read any kind of animal-related book, watch any kind of nature program, and talk about them for hours. She has had dogs and cats for as long as I have known her. I think I inherited my passion and love for animals from her, as well as Mum and Dad. She will always keenly discuss bird identification with me or what Fred has been up to or what my work at the vet clinic is like.

We used to visit nearly every school holiday, to horse-ride, go on big paddock walks, collect lemons, mushrooms, and almonds, to go cray-bobbing in the dam, and fly kites on windy days. There were toys from when Mum and her sisters were kids and we loved playing with those. We slept in Mum and Jude's childhood bedroom. Barndy always had a collapsing stack of National Geographic magazines by the TV, gluten-free bread, a big fruit bowl on the table, a bunch of logs by the small fireplace and an 'X' taped on the windows to stop the birds crashing into them.

Lai and I would always hope to stumble across some item around the house, like mini archaeologists from *Time Team*, that we used to watch when we were younger. There were relics of Old John's, artefacts from Mum and her sisters' youth, and prized possessions of Barndy's. One afternoon, I think it was rainy, Lai and I somehow pestered Barndy into getting out her old dresses. We tried them on (those that fitted) and listened to Barndy tell stories about the occasions she wore them. I was so excited, and at that stage going through a textiles obsession, and Barndy kindly gave them to me. For a year or so afterwards, I hung one of her salmon pink dresses off the wall of my bedroom. I still treasure them. I can see the glamour, the care and time that went into making them and feel the hopes and dreams of Barndy, before me, before Mum existed.

Barndy is also an avid reader. This year I've bought and lent her many books and she devours them quickly, writing letters and calling to talk about them. Kate volunteers in Rotary; they have a book sale every year. Last year, Mum and I said we would go and maybe we could get some for her. Barndy said firmly, 'Crime or historical fiction but no romance please'. Just like my sister Lai's taste in books. We brought her home a few and she chose delicately with the air of a connoisseur. I sent her a letter today, from the uni post office. It'll be a while till it reaches her though, and she has time to write back.

I loved the idea of amalgamating these traits, these life stories and mythologies of these women, my family. Adding it to the shape, the narrative of me.

They represent strength, independence, love, curiosity, resilience, and passion. It doesn't matter that society defined them as spinsters, aunts, wives, mothers, sisters, and daughters: to me, they are everything.

Who's the Foreigner?

Sandra Joy

Isn't it funny how we believe the things we are told without questioning them? This photo has been on a wall in every one of our family homes – and there's a lot of them, but that's another story. The verbal caption has always been that it's my mother, 'On the ship, coming out to Australia from England when she was twenty.'

Now, I know it's my mother. She was, after all, my mother for nearly fifty years. But that doesn't prove that everything I know about this photo, or her, is true.

Let's start with the fact that she's not actually on the boat. She's sitting on a railing on the dock. Maybe they took their luggage on board and came off again for a final photo. I don't know the sequence of events, but this photo is not taken 'on the ship' as I was led to believe.

I was eleven when I first noticed this photo. Mum was more than willing to reminisce about her homeland and the trip abroad. It was her twentieth birthday and, back then, it was customary for birthdays to be celebrated at the captain's table. So Mum, her older brother, and their parents were invited to dine in the prominent area of the dining hall – along with a bunch of strangers also born on that day.

As a teenage girl, this story took my imagination into fantasy land. For a long time, I dreamt of dining with the captain of a grand ship – though in my mind, we were all celebrating my twenty-first birthday and he fell in love with me. There's something way more romantic about my version of the story. But then, reality isn't always perfect.

Apart from the lie that was told, I like this photo of Mum. She's very pretty, and very happy. I have no doubt that the smile on her face would have been directed at a male. You see, my grandmother was the world's biggest flirt. She used to brag about having three dates on the same night. At least Mum pretended to be a prude my entire life. She always went to church, she would ignore me for days if I liked the wrong guy; and clothes, jokes, and manners were all very old-fashioned. And I know why – shame! That's right. Shame.

When I was in my early thirties, I came across some details that caused me to question the innocence of my mother.

Fact: My mother had her twentieth birthday on that ship, 21 January 1950.
Fact: My parents were married on 14 October 1950.
Fact: My oldest sister was born on 16 May 1951.

My mother moved to the other side of the world and, within nine months, travelled, met a man, fell in love, and got married. Back in 1950, that was okay, not uncommon. My sister was born, full-term, seven months later! Back in 1951, that was not okay, that was not common.

Three thoughts punished my mind. How did my strict Catholic mother get pregnant before she was married? How did I live in this family for thirty-two years and not know? And, what other secrets did my family keep stowed away from *the baby*?

I wonder what other adventures of immorality she experienced. Being so beautiful, it wouldn't be hard for her to attract men. Before coming to Australia, she was a London model. Apparently, she modelled for some high-class store; Harrods or something. I can't recall.

Mum raised her first two daughters to be truly fashionable young ladies. I have seen slides and photos of them when they were little girls, parading around in their lacy dresses and white frilly socks. When they weren't riding horses or wearing school uniforms, they wore the same style – and always had bags, gloves, and shoes to match.

I think the novelty wore off, or Mum finally accepted that London was a long way away, because, by the time she got to me, Mum no longer imparted her fashion skills. It must have been hard to recreate the London look when your makeup is rolling off from perspiration, or the flies are sticking to it. Living on the land, they only went to town once a month and, depending on the land, money grew short. Mum struggled, but never complained. She was strong. Instead, she turned her skills to making her home beautiful, and became very creative with the few resources she had.

So, the only deportment training I got was, 'You can wear lipstick when you're thirteen'. That was it. No training in fashion, style, or grooming. No array of clothes or accessories for me. So, I grew up not caring. It was all just to make you look good for other people anyway, and I was happiest in the countryside on my own.

When it came to learning about fashion, I missed the boat, but genetics speak loudly. Mum had a very narrow waist – typical of her time, and a feature of models back then. She passed that on to me, though I tend to hide it with the flabby results of junk food. My daughters both have it too, and they are stunners. Mum didn't teach them about makeup either, instead she just lectured, 'You're too young to wear that!' Thankfully, they grew up with friends who taught them all the girly stuff like clothes, makeup, hair, and accessories. It's funny that they both look like their nanna, yet they both look so different.

Now, my walls have only a few photos of my children and grandchildren and they are all beautiful in their own way. No-one has photos of me, I don't allow it. Photos hold memories of things that aren't true. These images are distorted or interpreted incorrectly. I don't like photos.

Unlike my mum, I have never travelled outside of this country. Yet, somehow, sometimes, I feel like I am the real foreigner.

Summer, 2020

Frankie Miller

We drove to Sydney in my little hatchback on a hot Saturday afternoon. You sat in my front seat, legs crossed, with a packet of wasabi peas. I like the way you cross your legs. With them tucked neatly away, it brings your face into focus. Your dark beard with flecks of blonde and red.

You read me the program for Students of Sustainability – SoS. Workshops on the green new deal, socialism, and anarchy. Panels on unions and anti-capitalism and the NSW bushfire crisis. On the freeway, the air was hazy orange, and smoke pushed its way through the air conditioner vents. The glove box in front of you was packed with face masks. A month before, I had no idea what N95 meant. Now I couldn't stop thinking about the smoke creeping into the lungs of people all across the state, its constant presence a reminder of loss. We had no idea that the fires were only a small taste of how it felt to live during a wide-scale human crisis. Soon the N95 masks would be switched for COVID-19 masks and hand sanitiser, and we would no longer be driving to conferences.

I remember how you spilled the wasabi peas all through the footwell as we pulled in for a rest stop. You kept saying that you 'pea'ed on the floor' and I laughed so hard that I almost peed my pants. I laughed so uncontrollably that you got flustered and self-conscious. I wanted to tell you that I only laughed so much because I enjoy you more than anyone else. Instead, I just said that I was overtired.

For a trip that we had set up to be platonic, little moments of intimacy were everywhere. My bra broke while I was driving. I shifted my body and the underwire shot out of its sleeve, stabbing my flesh. (Twelve years of wearing bras and mine chose to give up at that moment!) You had to stand outside the car while I scrambled free of the thing. I didn't have any spares (more than one bra when camping seemed extravagant), so I pulled a jacket over and tried to look nonchalant.

I had been nervous about this trip away with you. The way that I felt, and your long-term relationship, were a risky combination. Sally was in Adelaide so she couldn't come, but she was happy for us to go. SoS was a dream for both of us. And I was well-practised in muting my feelings. Six years of crushes on housemates and other people it wasn't practical to date had served me well. I was good at pretending.

We got to SoS at night. Campers were already sprawled across the lawns of Sydney University. Tents, tarps, mattresses in ute trays, and vans. I parked the car, and we picked our way through the groups, looking for a spot. I knew there were other people from Newcastle there – we were meant to travel with some of them. I had only met them once, though, and recognising masked faces in the dark is difficult. We picked a spot near the back of the lawn and put up our little one-person tents. Mine was blue, a gift from my parents for my eighteenth birthday. Yours was red. You bought it a few weeks before SoS and said you planned to get more into hiking.

'By yourself?' I knew you and Sally had a two-person tent.

'Yeah, well. I thought maybe you would like to go on a hike sometime.'

[pause]

'We could take a group.' You watched my face as you said that. I bit my lip and nodded.

The first night at SoS I was awake for hours. A busy road ran along the fence just behind our tents, and every truck that roared past felt like a threat. I wasn't surprised – I've suffered from insomnia since I was about eight years old. It doesn't matter how tired I am. When I have a lot to process, or I'm in a new environment, I'm hypersensitive to every noise and sensation. My hiking mat leaked, and I shifted around as it got progressively squishier. My back hurt. The trucks roared. I tried to think about all the workshops I was excited to go to. I brought back happy memories from the day gone past – how you spilled all the peas and our time chatting in the car. Now you were asleep about a metre away, separated by our canvas cocoons.

Breathe in. One, two, three, four.

Hold. One, two, three, four.

Breathe out. One, two, three, four.

By the time I fell asleep, the birds called out to each other across the orange sky.

When we woke up, all the tents were covered in ash. The wind was hot and smoky. It felt bad to be outside. We put our masks on and made our way up to the breakfast tent. There was a long table of food – polenta porridge, bowls of stewed fruit and sweet nuts, and plates of eggs, bacon, and toast. Many people at SoS were vegan, and so I was surprised by the animal products. But we learned that the meat was important for the First Nations groups present, and given their amplified status and respect at SoS, the vegans supplied cook-ups all week. So many tensions like this existed at SoS. I was surprised that it worked it all, to have hundreds of people co-exist like this.

I recognised a few people from Newcastle. Familiar faces from climate strikes. Lucas from uni. There were two young women that I once made coffee with for the Commons. It was when I first moved to Newcastle, and I tried to get into some volunteering roles. I turned up at the Wickham Croatian Club, not knowing anyone, in the middle of summer. When I found the coffee machine, both the girls were high, and the machine was broken. I tried to fix it for over an hour while they snorted powder off the table next to me. It made me smile, seeing them there. At the time when it happened, I was right out of my comfort zone. Now I was camping with them.

After breakfast, we said goodbye to each other and split off for different workshops. I felt relieved to have some space from you. I wanted to find my independence in this new crowd. That first morning at SoS, I remembered a book I used to read as a kid: *Are You My Mother?* I walked from workshop to workshop, wondering who I was becoming, who were 'my people'. I felt like a baby bird in a forest of wildlife: activists protesting on the frontline at Adani, waste-free vegans, prison abolitionists, feminists well-versed in political action.

It felt like everyone had a passion to live by. *Are you my people?* The energy and fervour were contagious. I wanted so badly to find a place to fit. Two years of uni and some of my own social justice advocacy had left me craving people who cared about the same things. Now I had found the veterans: those who not only had the ideas but were in the field, living it out. SoS was an ecosystem of change; each person focused on a particular area of justice, but willing to lend their energy wherever it was needed.

My first experience of social justice in practice was a Christian charity conference I went to with my dad when I was thirteen. It had talks on the environment, as well as what community development people were involved in overseas. I went to a talk run by a missionary based in Afghanistan. He told us about how they tried to build a well for a community there, but none of the locals used it. When his team discussed it with the community leaders, it turned out that the women who collected water would rather walk to the spring as it gave them time to spend with each other away from their families.

The women drew support from their walks with each other to the spring, and if they collected water from the well in the village they would miss out on this precious experience. As a wide-eyed thirteen-year-old, I discovered a new rage. *I* would be different. *I* would never force a well on a village. Almost ten years later, I still carry the same fire I discovered that day. But I've also created a trail of wells behind me.

You teased me because I complimented people to become friends with them. I did it that night at dinner. Two guys were behind us in the food queue. I told one of them that I liked his jacket, and he showed me all the pockets. Soon we were sitting with them on the grass with bowls of tofu and talking about climbing. They were from Newcastle as well. Cooper looked fresh from high school. He and his friend innocently went on a night-time adventure to their school. The cops turned up and body-slammed them, then put them in handcuffs.

'Oh yeah, that reminds me of my run-in with the cops!' I laughed.

'Go on then, what did you get done for?' Cooper leaned in.

I shared this story with the group:

I couldn't sleep so I went for a bike ride at midnight, in my pyjamas. I was living in a tiny town in Victoria, so the roads were completely dead at that hour. Then a single car approached from the other direction, did a U-turn, and sat behind me. I turned left into a side street, and the car turned too. I turned down another street and the car followed. My heart exploded, and I pedalled flat out to get away.

I crossed through an alleyway to change streets, but the car raced around and was already there when I arrived. My mouth was dry. My hands slipped from sweat on the handlebars. My house was only a few blocks away, but I had to ride over the main road to get to it. I hid in a driveway while the car went past slowly, and I forced myself to count to thirty. Then I pedalled as fast as I could on my one-speed bike, skinning my bare feet on the metal. The car found me. It sped up.

Closer. Headlights blasting my back.

Closer. I could feel the bonnet metres behind me.

Closer. My arms shook. Was it going to run me over?

When the car was only a metre away from my wheel, a police siren started. Blue and red cut through the headlights. I pulled my bike over and heaved air through my lungs, slumped over the handlebars. My whole body trembled.

The cops came alongside me and wound down the window.

'Oh God, it's the police. I thought you were trying to kill me, so I ran away and then you kept chasing and oh I'm so sorry, I was just going for a bike ride...' I stuttered through the words, still gasping for breath.

The cops, who were two old white guys, wouldn't meet my eyes. The driver turned the flashing lights off.

'Didn't mean to scare you, love. There have just been some break-ins around here lately.' He looked embarrassed while he said it.

'I'm in my pyjamas! On a vintage bike!'

The police left quickly after that. I wheeled my bike down to my house, ditched it in the yard and locked all the doors behind me. All my housemates were asleep, but I was awake for several more hours from the adrenaline.

I've gotten used to telling this story with self-deprecating humour. People usually laugh and wonder how these things happen to such an innocent-looking young woman. But this time when I looked around at the group, all I saw was your anger.

'Fuck the police! They're pigs! I can't believe they did that to you. It's disgusting.' The words spat out. Your eyebrows set low and heavy.

I had never heard you swear before. You said once that you hated how flippantly people used the F-word. Cooper and his friends added their support too.

'Frankie, I'm so sorry that happened to you. That sounds so traumatic.' You had calmed your voice so quickly, but I could still see the tension in your shoulders.

The emotion that you carried about my story took me by surprise. I was so used to people laughing at me, at the ridiculousness of the situation. For the first time, I properly realised the abuse of power that had shaken me so much.

I slept much better the second night. I woke up late after the sun had risen high, and the campsite was quiet. I opened my tent flap, and you were gone. I quickly put on some more clothes and washed my face with water from my drink bottle. *Shit, I've missed breakfast. Everyone must already be in the first session.* I organised my backpack for the day: a notebook, pens, face masks, and water. Then I saw you, walking down the slope to our tents, carrying my bowl.

'I thought I'd get you breakfast while you caught up on sleep.' You handed me the bowl with polenta porridge, fruit, and sweet nuts. I like the way your eyes are puffy in the morning. It makes you look gentle.

You had to leave that night, to get back to Newcastle for work. I watched you take down your tent, folding everything away with careful hands. Most people scramble around when they pack down a campsite. You had a bag and a place for every item.

Every time I looked at you, you met my gaze.

'I don't want to leave', you said quietly.

'I don't want you to leave either.' Neither of us moved. *It's just a friendship thing. We're both sad because that's what happens when you have an intense few days. I get sad after every camp.*

'It's crazy that we have spent so much time together and we're not sick of each other!' You broke the tension. Grinned at me and tightened your bag straps.

'Yeah. Huh. So weird!' *Not that weird.*

I cry easily. As we drove to the train station, I pressed my tongue to the roof of my mouth and clenched every muscle.

If you had just jumped out of the car – if I had just driven away quickly, we might have been saved by ambiguity. But I parked the car in the drop-off zone. I got out for a quick hug. And you leaned in and didn't let go. We stayed there by the side of the road, squeezing each other tightly, and it all clicked into place. We both knew what was going on. The laughter. The hiking plans. Our little tents next to each other. Your anger at the police. You bringing me breakfast. Clung together, we stood there, absorbing the significance. Then I let go, and you got on the train.

Cover Illustrator, Hannah McGregor, was born and raised in Canberra by parents who valued expression through creativity. Art has always been Hannah's passion so, after studying visual art throughout school, she moved to Newcastle (because of the beaches) to study a Bachelor of Communication, majoring in Journalism. The inspiration for the cover came from the idea that books and stories are an integral part of life, hence the three age groups – child, teenager and adult. The figures are deliberately not gendered. The lines represent the text that weaves us together, and forms us as individuals.

Editor, Dr Alexandra Lewis, is Lecturer in English and Creative Writing at the University of Newcastle, Australia. Until May 2019, she was Senior Lecturer at the University of Aberdeen, Scotland, where she was Director of the Centre for the Novel and Undergraduate Programme Coordinator of Creative Writing. Alexandra explores literature and psychology, trauma and memory, and her recent publications include the Norton Critical Edition of *Wuthering Heights* and an edited collection for Cambridge University Press, *The Brontës and the Idea of the Human: Science, Ethics, and the Victorian Imagination.* She serves on the executive committees of both the British and the Australasian Victorian Studies associations (BAVS and AVSA), as well as the International Advisory Board for the Collaborative Organization for Virtual Education (COVE), and is the President of the Hunter Writers Centre. Alexandra's poetry and fiction appear in *Causeway/Cabhsair; The Interpreter's House; Waymaking: An Anthology of Women's Adventure Writing, Poetry and Art; Victorians: A Journal of Culture and Literature; Axon: Creative Explorations* and *Southerly.*

Editor, Sandra Joy, is an emerging author with one self-published book and a series of children's books due for release this year. Sandra has a story published in *Beneath the Surface,* and won third prize in the Odyssey House Short Story Competition 2019. She is currently studying a Bachelor of Arts at the University of Newcastle where she is majoring in English & Writing. Sandra has been a member of the Hunter Writers Centre and the Fellowship of Australian Writers. She is a micro-publisher with the Australian Publishers Association. Sandra created the design and typesetting of this publication as part of an internship with the Hunter Writers Centre under the supervision of Dr Alexandra Lewis and Karen Crofts.

The Hunter Writers Centre is a not-for-profit organisation that supports literary artists in the Hunter region and beyond. Directed by Karen Crofts, the HWC is responsible for the Newcastle Short Story Award, the Newcastle Poetry Prize and the Grieve Competitions. The HWC provides sponsorship to local projects as well as internships to students of the University of Newcastle.

www.ingramcontent.com/pod-product-compliance
Lightning Source LLC
Chambersburg PA
CBHW030436120726
47903CB00003B/991